FROM THE
NANCY DREW FILES

ASSIGNMENT: *Just have a good time on a white water rafting trip with Ned, Bess, and George. Sounds like fun. But somebody in the group wants Nancy more than relaxed. This person wants her dead to the world.*

CONTACT: *Paula Hancock, the leader of the rafting expedition. Nancy has never seen her before. So why does Paula seem so familiar?*

SUSPECTS: *Max, a master rafter with a troubled past. He seems interested in Bess, but is it just a ploy?*

Tod, an immature loudmouth who plays with dangerous toys, like firecrackers—and switchblades.

Mercedes, Paula's cousin. She's watching every move Nancy makes—and rifling through Nancy's backpack.

COMPLICATIONS: *Both rafts are lost—one swept away, one sabotaged. Then Max and Paula disappear. Nancy has to get the group out of the wilderness alive. But that isn't easy when a maniac starts to stalk them—and the main target is Nancy Drew!*

Books in The Nancy Drew Files ® Series

Available from ARCHWAY Paperbacks

THE NANCY DREW FILES™

CASE ■ 6

WHITE WATER TERROR

Carolyn Keene

AN ARCHWAY PAPERBACK
Published by POCKET BOOKS
New York   London   Toronto   Sydney   Tokyo   Singapore

This book is a work of fiction. Names, characters, places and incidents are either the product of the author's imagination or are used fictitiously. Any resemblance to actual events or locales or persons, living or dead, is entirely coincidental.

AN ARCHWAY PAPERBACK *Original*

An Archway Paperback published by
POCKET BOOKS, a division of Simon & Schuster Inc.
1230 Avenue of the Americas, New York, NY 10020

Copyright © 1986 by Simon & Schuster Inc.
Cover art copyright © 1986 Enric
Produced by Mega-Books of New York, Inc.

ISBN: 0-671-73661-2

First Archway Paperback printing December 1986

10 9 8 7 6 5 4

NANCY DREW, AN ARCHWAY PAPERBACK and colophon
are registered trademarks of Simon & Schuster Inc.

THE NANCY DREW FILES is a trademark
of Simon & Schuster Inc.

Printed in the U.S.A.

IL 7+

WHITE WATER TERROR

Chapter

One

————————————

YOU'VE GOT TO be kidding," Bess Marvin said. She looked up from her seat in Nancy Drew's bedroom, where she was polishing her long, delicate nails. "I'm not going on any wilderness trip!"

"But, Bess, you'll love it," countered her cousin George Fayne.

Sitting cross-legged on her bed, Nancy Drew was engrossed in a puzzle and trying to block out the sound of her best friends' voices. The more difficult the puzzle, the better Nancy liked it. Thinking hard kept her mind limbered up for her more challenging work as a detective.

1

"Really, Bess, you *will* love it," George said again, seeing her cousin roll her eyes. "Lost River, the mountains, the trees, the birds—they're all yours, just for sitting comfortably in a rubber raft for a couple of days. You probably won't even have to paddle. The river will do all the work."

"I'll loathe it!" Bess exclaimed with a shudder. "Nancy," she implored, "tell George that this time she's really gone looney tunes."

Nancy put down her puzzle and looked at her friends. George, who had just come from her regular three-mile afternoon jog, was wearing a blue-and-green running suit that emphasized her athletic wiriness and made her look ready for anything. White water rafting was exactly the kind of thing that would turn George on. She loved any challenge. That was what made her so valuable to Nancy.

At the same time, rafting was exactly the kind of thing that would turn Bess *off*. At the moment, for instance, she was wearing a pair of tight purple stirrup pants and an enormous gauzy shirt, cinched with a thin gold belt. Her long, straw-colored hair curled loosely around her shoulders. It wasn't that Bess was afraid of adventure, and it wasn't that she was terribly lazy. She was just . . . well, Bess liked to do things the *easy* way. Maybe she *was* a bit timid, but she always enjoyed being where things were happening—and things always happened with Nancy around.

Nancy folded her arms and looked from one friend to the other with a grin. "Okay, George, start from the beginning," she said. "Tell us just how you managed to get *four* places on this rafting expedition. And where *is* Lost River, anyway?"

"I *told* you," said George, her dark eyes gleaming with excitement, "I don't even remember entering the contest. Maybe I did it when I bought those jogging shoes at the sporting goods store a couple of months ago. I vaguely remember filling out an entry blank for some sort of contest. Anyway, I got this letter yesterday from somebody named Paula Hancock, who owns White Water Rafting, notifying me that I'd won the grand prize in this national contest. Four places on a white water raft trip down Lost River, in the mountains of northwest Montana. They're even offering free plane tickets to Great Falls—the nearest city."

"Did the letter say anything about the kind of trip it might be?" Nancy asked. "I mean, there are rivers and then there are *rivers.*"

"According to the letter, Lost River is the ultimate white water challenge, full of rapids and falls. What a terrific vacation—and free, too. Anyway, we need a vacation," George said emphatically. "We've been working too hard."

Bess put the cap on her nail polish and shook her head. "George, you're crazy," she said. "Going rafting down some wild mountain river is no vacation—it's sheer torture!"

Nancy thought back to her last case, *Hit and Run Holiday*, a Florida "vacation" that had nearly gotten her killed. She had come to realize the importance of spending relaxed time with her friends. "We *do* need a break," she said.

"Yes," Bess said, brightening. "You're absolutely right, Nancy. But what we need is a break, not a breakdown. I vote for a long weekend at the beach. I know we were just in Fort Lauderdale, but what happened there certainly wasn't a vacation. I want to do nothing but lie in the sun and baste ourselves with tanning lotion. And when we're tired of the beach, we can go shopping." She threw Nancy a hopeful glance.

"Shopping!" George hooted, springing to her feet. "All you *ever* want to do is go shopping, Bess Marvin. Don't you have a larger purpose in life?"

Bess looked at George calmly. "Of course I do," she said with a twinkle in her eye. "Going out with a good-looking boy, for one. Or eating," she added.

George shook her head. "Funny. Ha, ha," she replied.

Nancy climbed off the bed and went to the window, where she stood looking out at the soft summer drizzle that was falling. A river trip might be fun, but she could see Bess's point. A beach vacation, a *real* one, would be relaxing, and baking under the hot sun on the shores of Fox Lake might be just the thing to take her mind off the detective business. But there was something else to think about. "You say you won a trip for four people?" she asked George again.

George nodded.

"Well, then, how about inviting Ned to go along?" Ned Nickerson was Nancy's longtime boyfriend. He was away at summer school just then, at Emerson College, and Nancy missed him. She had the feeling that her friendship with Ned could be the most important relationship in her life—if she could just make a little more time for it. But Ned, who had always been the most understanding guy on earth, seemed to be getting a little impatient with her. Nancy couldn't forget that during their case at *Flash* magazine, Ned had become involved with another girl. That hadn't lasted long, but . . .

The raft trip might be exactly the kind of thing to give the two of them plenty of relaxed, fun time together.

Nancy turned away from the window and continued thinking out loud. "Didn't Ned go on a couple of white water trips with his uncle a few years ago? He'd probably be a big help in case of an emergency or something."

"Emergency?" Bess went pale. "Like—like the raft tipping over?"

George looked at her scornfully. "Rafts don't 'tip over,' dummy. They *capsize*."

Bess turned a shade paler.

"Rafts don't capsize, either," Nancy said, patting Bess comfortingly on the shoulder. "They're too stable." She stretched and yawned. "Listen, Bess, if you want a vacation at the beach, go for it. But I've never been white water rafting, and it sounds like fun to me—if Ned can come along." She turned to George.

"Sure," George said enthusiastically. "Yeah. Ask Ned. We'll have a great time with him." She cast a sideways glance at Bess. "And with all the other boys."

"What other boys?" Bess asked.

"Are you kidding?" George replied. "The letter said there are six other kids coming along on the trip. Probably boys." She paused. "Rugged, masculine, plaid-shirted boys with broad shoulders and . . ."

"Well . . ." Bess said indecisively.

"Oh, come on," Nancy said. "It'll be great."

"Boys," George teased.

"Okay," Bess agreed. "I'll come."

* * *

"Bess Marvin has agreed to go white water rafting with you and George?" Ned said incredulously. He propped his feet up on Carson Drew's favorite ottoman.

Nancy's father was an internationally known criminal lawyer. He had taught Nancy a great deal of what she knew about detective work. At the moment, he was on one of his frequent trips, this one to the Middle East. Nancy missed him, but she wasn't alone. She had Hannah Gruen, the Drews' longtime housekeeper, who had been like a second mother to Nancy since the death of Nancy's real mother.

Nancy glanced at Ned. He was home for the weekend, and she was glad to see him. She was enjoying their cozy evening in the den watching TV.

"How'd you ever talk Bess into it?" Ned asked. "Lost River must be hundreds of miles from the nearest Neiman-Marcus."

Nancy dipped into a bowl of popcorn that Hannah had made for them before she'd gone to bed. "It wasn't easy," she admitted. She looked at Ned. He was wearing his light brown hair a little longer than usual and his face was darkly tanned. She wondered if he had been spending time at the college swimming pool—and if so, whether he'd been alone or . . .

She put her hand on his arm. "How about you?" she asked softly. "Could I talk you into a white water trip?"

"Me?"

"Yeah, you. As in you and me. And George and Bess, too, of course."

Ned pretended to look stunned. "I—I hardly know what to say. This is all so sudden. I . . ." Grinning, he ducked the pillow that Nancy tossed at him. "Yeah, sure, I'll go, Nan. Summer school will be over next week, and I won't have anything else to do."

"Well, I must say you don't sound all that wild about it."

Ned's grin faded. "I guess I'm just surprised," he said quietly. "Let's face it, Nancy. We've seen each other only two or three times in the last couple of months, and even then I was taking you away from your detective work —from something I felt you'd rather be doing. In fact, during a couple of your recent cases, I've gotten the idea that I wasn't a very important part of your life. We've patched things up, but who can tell whether the patch is going to be permanent? After all, maybe you've changed in the way you feel about me."

Nancy swallowed painfully, remembering how she had felt during the *Flash* case when she had seen Ned holding Sondra in his arms, when they had learned that Sondra's brother Mick was in trouble. "I guess that's a logical conclusion," she said, "but it's not the *right* one. I know I've been awfully busy, but that doesn't mean you're not important to me, Ned." She leaned back against the sofa pillows and clasped her hands behind her head. "You're *so* important to me that I can sort of relax knowing you'll be around, without having to worry about it a whole lot."

Ned leaned toward her and touched her cheek with the tip of his finger. There was a slight smile on his lips. "What you're saying is that you've been taking me for granted. Is that it?"

Nancy nodded regretfully. "I guess so. Maybe that's why I was so ready to accept George's offer of the raft trip. I think we need time together so you can help me figure out all over again just why it is I love you so much."

"We don't have to wait until we get to Montana for me to start working on that assignment," Ned said softly. He leaned closer and put his arms around her. "Let me give you a couple of reminders." He kissed her tenderly, then kissed her again. "Got it figured out yet, Detective Drew?"

Nancy relaxed into his arms. "No, not yet," she said. "Why don't you try again? When it comes to love, I'm a very slow learner."

At that moment, the telephone rang. Nancy sighed. "Somebody's got awfully poor timing," she said as she lifted the receiver.

"Nancy Drew?" The voice on the other end of the line was low and muffled.

9

"Yes?" Nancy said slowly, sensing that something was wrong.

The next words struck her with an icy coldness. Her stomach twisted into a frigid knot. "The trip your friend won is no prize," the voice said ominously. "If you know what's good for you, you'll stay home—and stay alive!"

Chapter

Two

Wʜᴀᴛ'ꜱ ꜱᴛɪʟʟ ɴᴏᴛ clear to me," Nancy told George and Bess the next day, leaning across the table at Bennie's Ice Cream Parlor, "is whether the phone call I got last night was a warning or a threat. I mean, I couldn't tell from the tone of voice whether the caller meant to threaten me with harm or keep me from getting hurt." She chewed her lip, puzzled. "I couldn't even tell whether the voice was female or male."

George dug into her favorite chocolate-mint ice-cream sundae. "Why in the world would anybody want to keep you from going on the trip?" she demanded. After a moment's hesitation, she turned to Bess. "That phone call . . . it wasn't *you*, was it?" she asked suspiciously.

Bess looked hurt. "I went to a concert last night and didn't get back until after midnight. Anyway, you know I wouldn't do something that ridiculous. If I wanted to keep you or Nancy from going on the trip, I'd try to convince you in person."

George sighed. "I know. Sorry."

Nancy took the last bite of her banana split, watching George intently. "Are you sure you've told us absolutely everything you know about the contest?"

"All I know is what's in that letter from Paula Hancock. I've tried and tried to remember exactly when I entered the contest, but I can't."

Bess smiled mischievously. "Well, then, maybe it would be better if we didn't go." She pushed her half-finished diet drink away, looking with longing at George's sundae. "The beach is awfully nice at this time of year."

Nancy looked at George. In the back of her mind was the growing conviction that there was something not right about the contest. But the phone call and George's inability to recall entering it were her only clues.

"I don't suppose you'd reconsider your decision to go?" Nancy asked half hopefully. "Maybe we could find another white water rafting trip, if you've got your heart set on that.

There must be others that would be just as exciting."

"Yes, but this is a *free* trip," George reminded.

Nancy and Bess exchanged long looks. "What about it, Bess?" Nancy asked.

"Well," Bess said reluctantly, "I'm not exactly thrilled by the idea of spending two whole days hanging on to a raft, getting drenched by icy water, and bouncing from one rock to another. But I hate to think of you out there on the river with some kook who makes weird phone calls." She shrugged. "You can count me in, I guess."

"That settles it, then," Nancy said with a grin, laying her spoon beside her empty dish. She felt good remembering that the three of them had always stuck together, even in tough times. Whatever happened, they weren't going to let George face the trip alone. Besides, it was already shaping up to be a very interesting vacation. "Lost River, here we come!" she exclaimed.

"Where in the world do you suppose we are?" Bess asked from the backseat of the rental car that Ned was driving. She leaned over and took the map out of George's hands. "Here, let *me* have a look at that map. Maybe I can find us."

Nancy leaned precariously over the front

seat. "The road just made another left turn back there," she said, pointing to the small hand-printed map that Bess was holding.

"Well, what do you think, Bess?" Ned asked, braking suddenly and twisting the wheel to avoid a granite boulder that had tumbled off a cliff and lay in fragments in the road. "Are we taking the right route?"

"It looks like we are," Bess said, grabbing frantically for the armrest as the car lurched sideways and threatened to go into a skid. "But who cares? The map doesn't have any route numbers or anything. If this is all we have to go on, Lost River is likely to *stay* lost." She thrust the map back at George. "You know, it's almost as if whoever drew this map *wants* us to spend the whole morning wandering around in the mountains."

"I hate to admit it, but Bess may have something there," George said, staring at the map with a puzzled frown. "And another thing. I can't figure out why nobody met us at the airport yesterday, the way the letter promised. You'd think that a company big enough to run a national contest would arrange to meet the grand-prize winner when she got off the plane."

Nancy nodded. "I wondered about that myself. What a start for a vacation!"

Actually, Nancy thought as she settled back into the car seat, it hadn't even begun to feel like a vacation yet. The four of them had rushed to the airport but waited several hours for a flight from Denver that was so bumpy it would have made an eagle airsick. In Great Falls, there was nobody to meet them—only an envelope containing a hand-drawn map. Scrawled on the bottom were unsigned instructions to pick up a rental car and drive to Lost River Junction that night.

But by the time a car was available, it was late. They had spent the night at the only place they could find—a motel next door to the airport, where jets seemed to plow through the bedrooms every hour on the hour. Dragging themselves out of bed, they were on the road by five o'clock—anxious to get to Lost River Junction before the rafts left at nine.

"Well," Ned said, rolling down the window and taking a deep breath, "now that we're here, I'm glad. Smell those pine trees. What a wilderness this is!"

It *was* a wilderness, Nancy thought. They hadn't seen a sign of civilization for miles. For the last half hour, the narrow two-lane asphalt road had twisted and turned upward into the mountains like a mountain-goat trail. At the moment it was zigzagging precariously across the face of a vertical rock cliff.

Above the cliff and on the other side of the creek, huge pine and spruce trees reached toward the clear blue Montana sky.

Even though it was the middle of July, the

15

breeze was cool and brisk and invigorating, not at all like the steamy, oven-hot summer weather they had left back home.

Nancy stretched and filled her lungs with the clean air. In spite of everything, she was glad they had come. She glanced at Ned's calm profile and his sturdy, capable hands on the steering wheel. She was glad to be with him. With Ned along to help her laugh, the trip hadn't seemed nearly so bad.

Bess looked out the window. "I suppose there are wild animals out there," she said in a worried tone.

"Right," agreed Ned. "Plenty of them." He grinned at Bess in the rearview mirror. "Black bears and cougars and mountain lions and rattlesnakes."

With a little moan, Bess shut her eyes tight and hunched down in the seat.

"You know, I'm really getting worried about how late we are," George said, glancing at her watch. "It's after eight o'clock, and we're scheduled to leave at nine. You don't suppose they'd start the trip without us, do you?"

"I don't think they'd leave without their grand-prize winner," Nancy consoled her. "They wouldn't dare. After all, you *are* the reason for this trip." She hesitated. If George were the reason for the trip, why had *Nancy* received the mysterious phone call?

"Anyway, I'm just as glad things got screwed

up with the rental car and that we didn't have to drive this road last night," Ned said. "With all these twists and turns, it's dangerous enough in broad daylight. I don't think we—"

"Ned!" Nancy yelled. "Stop!"

Just a few yards ahead of the front bumper, the road vanished into thin air.

Bess gasped.

Ned jammed his foot on the pedal, making the brakes squeal. "Oh, no!" George screamed. "We're going over!"

Chapter

Three

THE RENTAL CAR screeched around in a circle before skidding erratically to a halt. The four friends sat for a moment in stunned silence, once again staring at the sheer emptiness ahead. The road was completely gone, carried down the cliff and into the ravine by a massive rockslide.

"Ned!" Nancy exclaimed, her horror mixed with limp relief. "If you hadn't stopped when you did . . ."

"We're just lucky it was daylight," Ned said soberly.

Shuddering, Nancy peered down into the ravine where the slide had loosened enormous boulders and huge gray slabs of asphalt. "We would have been killed if we'd dropped down there!" She looked around. "Is everybody okay?"

Bess rubbed her head. A bump was beginning to appear where she had hit her head against the car window. "I think so," she said in a dazed voice. "Good thing we were wearing seat belts."

"But why isn't there a barricade across the road?" George asked, jumping out of the car and stepping cautiously to the edge of the drop-off.

"Maybe the slide just happened," Ned suggested.

Nancy got out and looked around. "I don't think so," she said. "There are signs of erosion down there, and even a few weeds in the rubble. I'd say this road has been out of commission for weeks, at least."

Bess came to stand beside Nancy. "What's that?" she asked, pointing to something orange half-hidden behind a pile of brush a dozen yards below. "Isn't that a barricade?"

George scrambled partway down the slope. "It *is* a barricade," she called. "It looks as if somebody tried to hide it!"

"You mean somebody tried to *kill* us?" Bess asked.

Nancy frowned. "I don't think we can draw that conclusion from the evidence," she said slowly. "All we know is that the road is out and the barricade is missing."

"That barricade was deliberately hidden," George corrected her breathlessly, climbing back up to the road. "There's no way it could have *accidentally* gotten covered up under all that brush." She shivered. "You know, Nancy, as Ned was saying a few minutes ago, if we'd driven up here last night after dark—the way we were supposed to—we wouldn't have stood a chance."

"That's true," Nancy said. "But we don't know that the barricade was removed just for *our* benefit. A road crew might have come to inspect the slide and forgotten to put it back up."

"Well, maybe you're right," Bess said, looking pale and shaken. "But I don't know. Between this and your phone call, Nancy, the whole thing looks really suspicious."

"You're right," Nancy agreed. "I'd say that we have to be on our guard."

"In fact," Bess said hopefully, "maybe we ought to reconsider." She turned to George. "Haven't we already had enough excitement for one trip?"

Ned had managed to turn the car around, and the girls got back in. "Well, what now?" he asked.

Nancy looked at the others. "Do you want to go back to Great Falls and take the next plane home? Or do we keep trying to find Lost River?"

"I want to get to the bottom of this thing," said George. "And I'm stubborn. I don't want to give up my prize." She looked around. "But just because I'm crazy, doesn't mean you all have to stay. I'll understand if anybody decides to go back home."

Bess heaved a sigh of resignation. "If George is staying, I guess I will, too."

Ned reached over and ruffled Nancy's hair. "I'm in this as long as you are, Nan," he said.

"In that case," Nancy said briskly, "we'd better find an alternative route. This road isn't going anywhere but down." She pulled a state highway map out of the glove compartment and began to compare it to the map they had been given. "I think I see how to get there," she reported after several minutes. "Let's go back to the last fork in the road and take a left. Then it looks like we take two more left turns—we'll be there in thirty or forty minutes."

"You're the detective," Ned replied cheerfully, and drove back down the mountain.

Thirty minutes later, they pulled up at Lost River Junction, a small cluster of weathered, tired-looking wooden sheds huddled under tall pine trees beside the road. As Nancy got out of the car, she saw that one of the sheds sported a crude sign that said White Water Rafting in crooked letters. The sign looked new, she noticed, in contrast to the old building. Down the hill, behind the building, she glimpsed a group of people standing on the bank of a river, next to two big rubber rafts.

"Looks like we've made it—finally," Ned announced, turning off the ignition.

"Fantastic!" George exclaimed. She got out of the car, her concern about the trip momentarily forgotten. "Listen to that river!"

"I hate to tell you guys this," Bess remarked, "but I hear roaring. *Loud* roaring."

"Right," Ned said, opening the trunk and beginning to pull out their gear. "Sounds like a pretty big falls not far away." Grinning, he handed Bess her duffel bag. "That's what white water rafting is all about, you know, Bess. Water falling over the rocks. It always makes a noise."

Bess took the bag, shaking her head.

Nancy slung her backpack over her shoulder and followed George to the river. She was wearing khaki-colored safari shorts and a red knit polo shirt, a sweatshirt tied around her neck. The sun felt warm on her shoulders.

"Hi!" George said, hailing a tall, thin-faced young woman who was standing beside one of the rafts. "I'm George Fayne. Can you tell me where to find Paula Hancock? She runs White Water Rafting."

The young woman looked up. Nancy couldn't tell whether she was surprised to see them. "I'm Paula," the woman said. She was in her early twenties, Nancy judged, wiry-thin and tense, like a nervous animal. "You're late. We expected you last night."

George bristled. "Yeah. Well, you might say that we've been victims of circumstance. That map you left for us at the airport took us on a wild-goose chase, and then we—"

Nancy stepped in. "Then we got lost," she interrupted smoothly, leaning her backpack against a tree. She threw George a warning glance. There wasn't any point in alerting Paula Hancock to their suspicions. If she had anything to do with the warning phone call or the missing barricade, Nancy didn't want to put her on her guard. "I'm Nancy Drew," she said, holding out her hand and studying Paula. "George invited me to come along."

"Glad to have you," Paula replied brusquely. She ignored Nancy's hand. She had odd amber eyes, Nancy noticed, cold and remote.

Nancy shivered as though somebody had dropped an ice cube down her neck. "Have we . . . have we met?" she asked hesitantly. Those eyes—where had she seen them?

Paula straightened up. "I don't think so," she said more casually. "Not unless you've been up here before."

23

"No," Nancy said. "This is my first trip to Montana." She was sure she had never met Paula, but she couldn't shake the feeling that she knew those eyes.

Paula turned to a dark, good-looking young man in a faded blue denim work shirt and jeans, who was loading a radio into one of the rafts. "Max, come and meet our grand-prize winner, Georgia Fayne. Max is an expert river-rafter," she said, turning back to George and Nancy. "He'll handle one of our rafts. I'm taking the other."

"It's not Georgia, it's *George,*" George said, shaking Max's hand. "This is my friend Nancy. And Bess," she added as the others came up, "and Ned. We're really looking forward to the trip. Ned's been on a raft trip before, but the rest of us are novices."

"Glad to meet you," Max said. A long, hairline scar cut across the corner of his square jaw, giving him a lopsided look. He smiled at Bess as he shook her hand, his dark eyes glinting appreciatively. "Real glad."

Nancy looked at Max closely. The voice on the phone could just as easily have been a man's voice as a woman's. In her experience, it was better to consider everybody a candidate for suspicion. And Max looked like a likely one. But then, so did Paula. Since she was the owner of White Water Rafting, she must have been responsible for the contest—and for that killer map. Nancy decided to watch both of them closely.

Paula glanced at the sleeping bags and packs that Ned was carrying. "Go ahead and stow your gear in Max's raft," she commanded. "The sooner we get started, the better." She frowned at Max. "Did you check the batteries before you loaded the emergency radio?"

Max nodded. "Sure thing," he said carelessly. "Can't be out on the river with a radio we don't trust, can we?"

"Hi! Let me show you where to put those." A pretty girl walked over to Ned and took one of the sleeping bags from him. She was petite and willowy, and her ash-blond hair swept softly over her shoulders. "I'm Samantha," she told him in a soft southern drawl. "But my friends call me Sammy."

"Well . . . sure," Ned said, with a shrug and a quick glance at Nancy. He followed Sammy to the raft. Paula went along, too, calling out instructions for stowing the gear.

Nancy looked at George. "Maybe we should meet some of the others," she suggested, pointing to a group of kids standing beside one of the rafts.

"Okay," George said. "I'm looking forward to—"

George didn't get to finish her sentence. Suddenly the air around them exploded in a series of sharp, staccato sounds, like gunshots fired in rapid succession. Somebody was shooting at them!

Chapter
Four

GET DOWN!" NANCY yelled, pulling George with her in a wild dash for the shelter of a nearby tree. The gunshots continued, echoing through the trees. Crouching low, Nancy waved frantically at several other kids who were still standing beside the rafts, out in the open. "Get down!" she yelled. "Somebody's shooting!"

"Oh, come on," one of the girls called back. "That's not a gun. It's just Tod and Mike shooting their dumb firecrackers." The explosions stopped suddenly and there was absolute quiet, except for the sound of the falls.

"What?" Nancy stood up and looked around. "Tod and Mike? Firecrackers?"

"Those two clowns love practical jokes," the girl explained, coming over to them with a smile. "Firecrackers under a trash can. They've been at it all morning." The girl was short, thin, and dark-haired, and she had a nervous intensity that reminded Nancy of Paula.

Nancy let out the breath she'd been holding. She felt her pulse slow down to its normal rate.

"Hah! We sure scored one on you, didn't we?" The boy who came running to Nancy and George looked very pleased with himself. He was short and stocky and wore a pair of faded cutoffs and a plaid flannel shirt with the sleeves rolled up. "I'm Tod. And this is Mike." He pointed to the boy who had followed him over. The accomplice was tall and thin, his legs looking like pipestems in his frayed cutoffs.

"Listen, you guys, I don't think it was funny at all," George protested, coming out from behind the tree. "You scared us to death!"

But Nancy just said mildly, "Yeah, you sure scored one. We *were* pretty scared." Were Tod and Mike really immature enough to think it was *funny* to frighten people like that?

"Well, I've got to say this," Mike observed, looking at Nancy appraisingly. "You sure think fast and act fast—for a girl." He grinned and shuffled his feet. Maybe, thought Nancy, he was shy.

The dark-haired girl spoke up. "I'm Mercedes." She pointed to two others who had come up behind her. "This is Linda and this is Ralph. I guess you've already met Sammy," she added, looking toward the raft, where Sammy was standing close to Ned, talking animatedly with him.

Nancy followed her glance. "Yes," she said wryly, wondering if Sammy was going to be another Sondra—or worse. "We've already met Sammy. She seems very . . . friendly. And helpful."

"Yeah, that's Sammy, all right." Tod nudged Mike. "*Very* friendly. And *very* helpful."

Linda was a delicate, fragile-looking girl with a narrow, pointed face that reminded Nancy of a princess in a fairy-tale book. Ralph, slender with intense black eyes, was probably the scholarly type. He seemed a little out of place next to Tod and Mike, both of whom looked as if they'd grown up in the woods. Nancy listened carefully to them as Mercedes introduced them, trying to detect any trace of the voice that had made the phone call. But the week-old memory of a muffled voice wasn't much to go on.

However, after a few minutes of conversation, Nancy had found out some essential details about their companions. Except for Nancy, Ned, Bess, and George, everyone seemed to be from the area, which struck Nancy as a little odd. Hadn't George said that the contest was *national?* If that was true, why weren't there any winners from other parts of the country?

Mercedes turned out to be Paula's cousin, a fact which didn't surprise Nancy, given the nervous energy they seemed to share. Linda and Ralph were both from Great Falls and appeared to be close friends—also not surprising, Nancy thought, since they, too, seemed alike, both quiet and shy. Tod and Mike came from a nearby small town and, according to them, were experienced rafters.

"There's not much about Lost River that we don't know," Tod bragged. "We've made half a dozen trips down it in the past couple of years. We could handle these rafts ourselves, without any trouble—and all the gear, too. Like the radio, for instance. Isn't it a beauty?" He jerked his thumb toward Mike. "Mike here is the expert on this baby. Right, Mike?"

Mike nodded. "Yeah, I guess so," he said. "Radios are my hobby."

"Is rafting dangerous?" George asked excitedly. She sounded as if she wished it were, but she wasn't sure she should. She cocked an ear. "It *sounds* dangerous," she said, listening to the thundering of the falls.

Mike shrugged. "Not if you know what you're doing." He cast a meaningful glance at Max, who had just joined the group and was busily talking to Bess. "Of course, if you're careless or just plain dumb, somebody's going to get hurt—or worse." Nancy thought that Mike sounded as if he were challenging Max's raft-handling ability. She wondered if he knew something about Max that the others didn't.

Max turned to Mike. "Lost River is *always* dangerous," he said flatly. "It doesn't matter how much skill you have. The worst thing you can do is take it for granted."

Linda and Bess looked frightened. "You mean the rafts aren't safe?" Linda said haltingly.

"A raft is always safe as long as it is right-side-up and everybody stays on it," Mike replied, with another challenging look at Max.

"Do they capsize often?" Bess asked, glancing at George and putting special emphasis on the word *capsize*. Nancy hid a smile. Bess was learning the vocabulary.

"Hardly ever." Max tipped his cap toward the back of his head.

"As long as you don't get careless," Tod put in. "If you do . . ."

"Right," Max said, avoiding Mike's eyes. He put his hand casually on Bess's arm. "Listen, Bess, if you're scared, ride along with me, and I'll show you what to watch out for. That way, you'll understand what's going on."

A happy smile lit Bess's face. "Sure," she said. "I'd love to."

Nancy and George exchanged worried looks. Why did Bess have to give away her heart on a moment's notice? They'd have to talk with her first chance they got and warn her.

For the time being, Nancy just wanted some answers to the questions that had been bothering her all along. How much did the others know about the contest? George couldn't remember entering it—could they? She turned to Linda. "So," she said, "another lucky winner. Tell me how *you* won the contest."

Linda shook her head. "You know, it's funny," she replied timidly. "When the letter from Paula Hancock came, I was completely surprised. I couldn't even remember *entering* a contest."

"Me, neither," Ralph volunteered. "Linda and I have talked about it, and neither one of us can figure out exactly how we got here."

Nancy looked at Mike and Tod. "What about you?" she asked.

Tod shrugged. "Who knows? I don't remember entering, but I might have. You know how it goes. When you see a contest at a store or something, you always put your name in the box. I figure that's what happened here. I probably entered it at the sporting goods store."

"Yeah," Mike put in. "When we got the

letters we couldn't remember exactly." He glanced around with a slightly puzzled look on his face. "In fact, neither of us could remember ever hearing about White Water Rafting, which is kind of funny, since we live so close by. It must be a new company."

"What does it matter how any of us got here?" Mercedes interrupted quickly, stepping forward. "We're all going to have the time of our lives—and White Water Rafting is paying for the whole thing! What's the point of asking all these questions?"

Before Nancy could answer, Paula hurried over to them, followed by Ned and Sammy. Nancy noticed that Sammy was casting very interested glances at Ned—and that Ned didn't seem at all reluctant. In fact, he was laughing at something Sammy had said.

Nancy gave an inward sigh. This was supposed to be a time when she and Ned could get reacquainted with each other. But with all the distracting questions and frightening events, it was beginning to look more like a case than a vacation. And Sammy was giving her something else to worry about.

"Okay, everybody. The rafts are loaded," Paula announced. "Now, I'm going to give you a few important instructions." She pointed toward the rafts, big rubber boats eighteen or twenty feet long and five or six feet wide. One was pulled up on the shore, the other was in the river, moored with a line.

"See those wooden platforms toward the stern, where the oars are? Max and I sit on them. Everybody else sits down inside the raft—no standing up, no clowning around. Wear your life vest all the time, no matter how uncomfortable it gets. Pick a buddy—if anything happens, keep your eye on your buddy and be responsible for each other." She looked around the group. "Any questions?"

When nobody answered, she said, "Okay, then, let's get going. The first major falls is only about fifty yards downstream. It's too dangerous to raft over, so we'll take the sluice to the left to avoid the worst of it. It's a sort of natural waterslide along the left shore, and it's much tamer than the falls. We know what we're doing, but it'll be rough going for a few minutes, so hang on." She eyed Nancy. "I'm assigning you to the raft on the right, Nancy. Climb aboard. There are some life vests stowed under the platform."

The raft was moored to the shore with a line tied to a stake stuck in the mud. Nancy pulled it toward her and clambered aboard, scrambling awkwardly over a small heap of supplies and equipment stowed in the middle of the raft. The raft bobbed violently under her weight, and she grabbed for a handhold. She could feel the current tugging against the mooring line as if it were trying to tear the raft free.

Suddenly the line gave, jolting her to her knees as the raft swept away. The turbulent current of Lost River was pulling Nancy directly toward the falls!

Chapter

Five

"NANCY! HANG ON!" she heard Ned shout.

The roar of the falls was growing louder. Grabbing for the oars, Nancy figured she had only fifty yards or so before she went over, and Paula had said that the falls were too dangerous for the raft to negotiate.

So, Nancy told herself, she'd have to hurry—do *something* so she wouldn't be dashed to death on the rocks.

Glancing up, she saw Ned racing along the riverbank. Max and George were running hard behind him. Ned carried a coil of rope. "Row!" he called. "You've got to get out of the current!"

Nancy swallowed nervously. The ten-foot oars felt heavy and awkward, and her knuckles were white from gripping them so hard.

"Swing the raft toward the left!" Max yelled, coming up behind Ned. "Push on the right oar and pull on the left!"

Bracing her feet, Nancy followed Max's instructions. The oars cut into the water. After a moment, the raft swung left, responding like a huge, sluggish whale. She began to row forward, toward the bank. But the current was much too strong.

"She'll never make it!" Bess yelled.

"Maybe we can get a line to you," Ned shouted. "Row to the left. The current's not so bad closer to the shore."

Mustering all her strength, Nancy pulled hard on both oars, trying to keep the bow of the boat moving left. She frantically looked for a life vest, but couldn't see one on the raft. If she fell in the water, she couldn't fight the current.

"Closer!" Ned ran along the bank to keep up with the raft. "The rope's too short. I can't reach you!"

Then Nancy remembered the sluice. Hadn't Paula said something about avoiding the falls by taking it? She peered downriver. There, near the left shore, was the natural waterslide, funneling the river along safely in a milky white froth, neatly avoiding the falls. "I'm heading for the sluice!" Nancy shouted to Ned. She was still rowing energetically, but her endurance was fading.

Despite her aching shoulders, Nancy held on. She focused every ounce of will on getting away from the pull of the falls.

Finally, the swifter current seemed to yield to her power. Almost magically, the raft swung toward the sluice, and now, at least, she had a chance.

On shore, Ned vaulted over a fallen tree, still trying to keep pace. "There's a sandbar ahead," he called. "Beach the raft on it!"

For an instant the raft was balanced on the lip of the long slide. Nancy raised the oars and lay far back, icy water spraying her face. With a giant *whoosh!* the raft dropped over the edge. Nancy squeezed her eyes shut and prayed. It was like being on the giant waterslide at the amusement park—but without any guarantee of safety.

The raft was completely out of control. It hit the turbulent water at the foot of the sluice with a giant splash, completely drenching Nancy. Then it bobbed along more quietly as she grabbed for the oars again and began to steer toward the sandbar. There was Ned, with George and Bess. He still had the rope in his hand.

"Here," he shouted, tossing the end of the rope to her. She grabbed it and let him pull her ashore.

When the raft was safely beached, Nancy stumbled out. Ned caught her in his arms and held her for a minute, shivering.

"Well," Max said with a grin as he caught up to them, "that wasn't exactly the way we planned to get started. But now you know what rafting is all about."

"We've got to get you some dry clothes, Nancy," Bess added.

"Forget it," Paula said, joining them. "Before the day is over, *everybody* will be wet." She frowned at Nancy. "Where was your life vest? How come you didn't put it on?"

"Life vest?" Nancy asked. "There weren't any in the raft!"

Paula shrugged. "I guess they hadn't been loaded yet." She looked around at the rest of the group that had gathered. "So now you know. Accidents are a matter of routine on the river. You've got to be prepared for the worst."

Accident? Nancy wasn't convinced. She bent over the raft to examine the mooring closely. The stake was still attached to the line.

"What do you think?" Ned whispered to her. "Was it done deliberately?"

Nancy straightened up just in time to catch Paula's intense gaze. Had she heard Ned's question?

"I can't be sure," she replied in a low voice. She took Ned's arm and walked casually away. "The mooring line hadn't been cut or damaged.

It looks like the stake just pulled out of the mud. So maybe it *was* an accident."

"The other raft was pulled up partway on the shore," George pointed out, hurrying to them. "That looks like a safer way to load people. And after the missing barricade . . ."

"Yeah, I know," Nancy said grimly. "It's beginning to look like we're awfully accident prone."

Half of the group, including Linda and Ralph, went back upstream to board Max's raft. Linda seemed very frightened and kept saying that she wanted to back out, but Ralph put his arm around her comfortingly, and after a few minutes she calmed down. Nancy could hear Bess talking to Max. "Are you sure the raft is safe?" she was asking anxiously.

"Couldn't be safer," Max assured her confidently. "There are only two things that can destroy one of these rafts. One is to hang it up on a sharp rock. The other is to take a knife to it." He laughed. "We're going to make sure the first thing doesn't happen. And I can't imagine anybody being stupid enough to do the second. Can you?"

Nancy and George, Ned, Tod, and Sammy stayed behind on the sandbar to board Paula's raft. As they got on, Sammy managed to settle down cozily in the bow next to Ned.

"Paula said to choose 'buddies,'" she reminded him, edging closer to Ned. "I choose you!"

Ned cast a quick glance at Nancy, who was sitting farther back in the raft. Nancy shrugged. She wasn't thrilled about the idea of Sammy being Ned's "buddy," but she wasn't going to make a big thing about it.

"Well, okay," Ned said. He seemed flattered. "For now, anyway."

"Oh, that's just wonderful!" Sammy exclaimed happily. She pulled her life vest over her head. "Will you show me how to buckle this, Ned?"

Nancy turned away. The last thing she needed was giggly Samantha making a play for Ned!

"Don't worry," George whispered, squeezing Nancy's hand. "Ned's not going to be taken in by an airhead like that."

"I don't know," Nancy said doubtfully. Ned looked as if he were enjoying himself, bent close to Sammy, fastening the straps of the life vest around her slender waist. "She *is* awfully pretty."

At that moment, Max's raft came over the sluice, everyone screaming at the top of their lungs. It bounced into the pool with a giant splash. "Okay, here we go," Paula said to Nancy's group. She and Tod gave the raft a push off the sand and into the current. "Everybody hang on!"

With Paula seated on the platform and rowing strongly, the raft swung slowly out into the current and then picked up speed, following Max's raft. Since it was nearly ten o'clock, the sun was high overhead, but the air was still cool. Nancy settled back comfortably. This stretch of Lost River was broader and deeper, and for the next half hour or so, the rafts rode smoothly and easily. Pines and spruce trees crowded both banks. High against the blue sky a hawk soared powerfully, and somewhere deep in the woods a woodpecker drummed a staccato beat.

"Isn't this terrific?" George sighed. She was wearing her binoculars around her neck and suddenly raised them to her eyes. "I think that's a bald eagle in that tree!" she said, awed.

"I wouldn't be surprised," Tod said casually from his spot next to Nancy.

"I thought they were rare," Nancy said.

Tod shrugged. "To the rest of the country, maybe. Not around here." He grinned. "One of my buddies had one for a while."

George's eyes got round. "A bald eagle? You mean as a pet?"

"Yeah, a little one. For a while. He had a coon, too, but it got to be a pest." He grinned broadly, and Nancy noticed that he was missing a tooth. "Made a nice cap."

"A cap?" Nancy asked in disgust. "He skinned it?"

"Naw." Tod grinned. *"I* skinned it." He pulled a six-inch switchblade out of his pocket and began flicking the blade in and out. "Butchered and skinned it, all with this knife." A flick of his hand brought the blade out again. "Sharp as a razor." He grabbed Nancy's arm and turned it over. "Bet I could kill a bear with this knife," he boasted, touching the sharp-honed blade to the blue veins of her wrist.

Nancy jerked her arm away, staring at Tod. His eyes looked innocent, but she had seen plenty of criminals who looked that way. She would have to keep a watch on him.

But at the same time, she had the feeling that several people were keeping a watch on *her.* She could feel Paula's amber eyes constantly on her. And from the other raft, both Mercedes and Max seemed to be watching her, too. Why?

After another hour and a half, Paula began to paddle the raft out of the current, toward shore. "Lunch break," she called. She beached the raft on the sandy bank, where a small creek came gurgling out of a narrow canyon to join the larger river.

Paula pointed. "There's a huckleberry patch a little way up that creek, under those willows. If you've never eaten wild huckleberries, why don't you go try some while Max and I fix lunch?" She handed over a bucket for the berries.

"I'm ready for some huckleberries," George said enthusiastically. "It's been a long time since breakfast back at that motel."

"Oh, Ned, this sounds like such fun!" Sammy exclaimed, clutching Ned's arm.

Ned cast a look at Nancy, but Nancy glanced stubbornly away. If he was going to fall for Sammy's ridiculous little game, let him! She watched him follow Sammy up the creek. Then she and the others trailed behind. The huckleberry patch was fragrant. Most of the kids feasted while they picked, and their faces and hands were stained with purple huckleberry juice. Bess sighed contently, bending over the dense bushes next to Nancy.

"Almost as good as the beach?" Nancy teased.

"Well, not quite," Bess admitted. "Still . . ."

Suddenly she was startled by the crackling twigs and the loud rustle of leaves nearby. Bess looked up in alarm. She clapped her hand to her mouth. Then she gave a loud, shrill shriek.

"What is it?" cried Nancy.

Bess gasped.

Nancy whirled around, and there, rising up before her on its hind paws, its teeth bared in a fierce snarl, was a huge black bear!

Chapter

Six

NANCY'S HEART NEARLY stopped beating as she looked, terrified, into the ferocious mouth of the bear, its teeth gleaming yellow against the darkness of its throat. For a moment, like a slow-motion scene in a horror movie, the bear seemed to tower over them, claws outstretched, mouth open, roaring.

Ned and Sammy were a dozen paces away, picking berries. Ned looked up, horror in his eyes. "Get back, Nancy!" he shouted.

"Ned!" Sammy cried as Ned crept toward Nancy. "Don't leave me!" She lunged for him, and they both fell sideways into the berry bushes.

"Scat! Shoo! Beat it! Get out of here, you stupid bear!" Suddenly Max was in front of Nancy and Bess, between them and the bear, clapping his hands and shouting. He snatched off his cap and flapped it under the bear's astonished nose. "Scram! Shoo! Go!"

For a moment, the bear hesitated. Then its surprise turned to panic and it wheeled, dropped to all fours, and loped off into the bushes without a backward look.

"Wow!" Bess sank down weakly onto a nearby boulder and mopped her forehead with the tail of her blouse. Her face was white. "I have never been so scared in all my life!"

Nancy let out the breath she had been holding. "Me, neither!" she said.

"Are you all right?" George rushed up, looking anxious.

"Max saved us," Bess whispered, gazing at him adoringly. "He scared a grizzly bear away just by yelling at it."

"That wasn't any grizzly," Max said as Tod dashed up, panting. "And it wasn't very big, either. When you're scared, things have a way of seeming bigger than they are. It was just an ordinary black bear, probably no more than a yearling, taking a morning sunbath and a berry break at the same time." He laughed. "When it comes right down to it, *we're* the ones who are trespassing. This is *his* berry patch, you know."

"I wish I'd been there," Tod said. He glanced

at Max. "That ol' bear wouldn't have been able to walk away when I got through with him."

"Don't be stupid," Max snapped. "You don't want to go messing around with bears—not with that toy knife of yours."

Nancy stepped between them. "We're just glad this is all over," she said, interrupting Tod. "And that nobody got hurt."

Tod threw them a baleful look and turned angrily away. "You think you're so smart," Nancy heard him say under his breath as he stormed past her.

She stared after him, puzzled. Was his remark aimed at her or at Max?

Bess looked around. "Where's Ned?" she exclaimed. "I heard him shouting just a moment ago, but I haven't seen him since before the bear attacked."

"Here I am," Ned said. He limped up to them, covered with scratches. Sammy was still sitting in the berry bushes with a sullen look on her face. "I tried to help, but I didn't quite make it." He threw a disgusted look over his shoulder at Sammy. "I'm sorry," he said.

Nancy couldn't help chuckling. "By the looks of you, you'd have been better off meeting up with the bear."

Ned flashed a weak smile, then grew redfaced. Nancy knew he was embarrassed about Sammy, and that it was time to help him feel better about what had happened.

"That's okay," she said comfortingly. "It's the thought that counts. I know you would have helped if you could have."

Ned came closer. "Forgiven?" he asked softly.

"Nothing to forgive," Nancy replied, and Ned's face broke into a wide grin. Sammy scrambled to her feet and walked away without a word, her face stormy. Nancy looked after her. She didn't think Sammy was the kind to bear a grudge, but it might not be a bad idea to keep an eye on her.

Max called for attention. "Listen, kids, when you're out in the woods, make a lot of noise to let the bears and other big animals know that you're not trying to sneak up on them. If you happen to surprise a mama bear when she's out for a stroll with her cub, or if you manage to get between a mama and her cub, you're asking to have a tremendous bite taken out of you."

"Is that how you got that scar on your face?" Bess asked curiously. "A bear?"

Max ran his hand across his jaw. "No," he said brusquely. "I got it in a rafting accident." He picked his cap up off the ground and jammed it on his head. "Got to go see how lunch is coming along," he said, and left.

Bess looked longingly after him. "I wonder what kind of accident it was," she said with a sigh. "I'll bet he rescued somebody, or something like that."

"Well, it's obviously something he doesn't want to talk about," Nancy said. It concerned her that Bess was developing a giant crush on Max—the kind of crush that could easily blind her to the real person.

Apprehensively, Nancy remembered how Mike and Tod had implied that there might be something wrong with Max's raft-handling abilities.

"Listen, Bess," Nancy said, as they started together down the path to the river. "I need to say something to you about Max."

"Isn't he wonderful?" Bess asked with a dreamy look in her eyes, her words bubbling over. "You know, I wasn't sold on this trip in the beginning. But *now*, well, you should see Max handle the oars on that raft, Nan. He knows exactly what he's doing. And those muscles—wow!"

Nancy gave her a cautioning look. "You know, Bess, maybe it isn't a good idea to let yourself fall head-over-heels for this guy. There are some pretty weird things going on on this trip, and Max could be involved in them."

"He isn't that kind of person," Bess said flatly. "He saved us from the bear, remember? I mean, he could have let the bear attack us, and that would have taken care of us for good."

Nancy flung up her hands in cònfusion. "I don't know. Maybe the bear wasn't part of the plan, and he just reacted spontaneously. Or maybe I'm entirely wrong and he's not involved at all. But there's something awfully strange here, and I don't want you to get hurt, that's all."

They reached the end of the trail, where it opened out onto the sandy beach. "Well, I appreciate your concern for my feelings," Bess said huffily, "but I'm a big girl now. I think I can be trusted to know what's good for me and what isn't. I—"

Nancy put a hand on Bess's arm. "Shh," she said. The rafts had been pulled up on the deserted beach about ten yards ahead. Everybody else was off picking berries or making lunch farther down the beach, or walking in the woods. Everyone except Mercedes. She was bent over the pile of gear stowed in the middle of Paula's raft.

"What's she doing there?" Bess wondered. "Hey! She's going through someone's pack."

But Nancy was already on the beach, marching forward. "That's not anybody's pack," she said grimly. "She's going through mine!"

Chapter

Seven

Nᴀɴᴄʏ ᴡᴀʟᴋᴇᴅ ᴛᴏᴡᴀʀᴅ the raft, Bess following her closely. "Can I help you, Mercedes?" she asked pleasantly.

Mercedes straightened up and jumped back. "Help me?" she stammered. "No, I . . . I was just looking . . . in Paula's pack. For—for some sunscreen."

Nancy pointed. "The pack you're looking in just happens to be mine."

"Yours?" Mercedes looked down. She gave a nervous little laugh. "How silly of me. Of course it's yours. It even has your name on it. I don't know what I was thinking. I'm so sorry. I hope you don't think that I—"

"Well, as a matter of fact—" Bess began hotly.

"No, of course not," Nancy interrupted, overriding her friend. "I'm sure it must be easy to make a mistake like that."

Nodding, Mercedes backed away, then turned and hurried up the beach.

"Now, what was that all about?" Bess asked, turning to Nancy. "Mercedes *knew* what she was doing."

Nancy looked quickly through her pack. "Nothing's missing," she said. "But you know, in a funny way this doesn't surprise me. I've had the feeling all morning that Mercedes has been watching me."

"Could she have anything to do with the mooring line?" Bess asked.

"I suppose so. But so could almost anybody else—especially Paula and Max."

"Now, wait a minute," Bess said. "I still don't think that Max—"

Nancy held up her hand. "Finding a criminal is different from defending him in the courtroom, Bess. Out here, everybody is guilty until we know beyond the shadow of a doubt that they're innocent. No exceptions."

Bess sighed. "Well, I still don't think he did it," she muttered.

Fifteen yards down the beach, everybody was beginning to gather around the fire that Paula had built. She and Max had spread sandwiches on a towel, along with apples and bananas and bags of chips. George and Ned were there, helping themselves, when Nancy and Bess arrived. The four friends sat down on the sand with their lunches, a little apart from the others.

". . . and then she just walked away," Nancy said in a low voice as she finished telling George and Ned how she and Bess had caught Mercedes rifling her pack. On the other side of the fire, Sammy and Mercedes were deep in conversation. Nancy wished she could hear what they were saying.

"Mercedes is Paula's cousin, isn't she?" George asked quietly. "Do you think it's possible that Paula or Max asked her to look through your pack?"

"At this point, there's no way to know—she might even have done it on her own," Nancy said, ignoring the look Bess gave George. "You know, this is really an odd situation. Usually when I'm working on a case, I know what kind of crime we're dealing with—and the clues usually make some sort of sense."

"Yeah," Ned agreed. He trailed his fingers idly up and down her spine. "But this time, there are just these crazy things that keep happening. Since there's no real crime, it's hard to know whether any of the things are tied together."

53

"It's all so bizarre," Nancy said, moving a little closer to Ned. The touch of his fingers tingled through her. At that moment, Sammy looked up and saw what Ned was doing. She glared at him and then turned back to Mercedes.

George pushed a brown curl out of her eyes. "You know, I'm beginning to think that maybe the most bizarre thing of all was my winning the contest in the first place."

Nancy nodded. "None of the other kids can remember entering the contest, either. It's as though this whole thing were invented." A shadow fell across her shoulder and George's cautioning glance made Nancy stop talking.

"So you've had your first taste of rafting," Max said, squatting down next to Bess. "Did you like it?" His voice was friendly, but his eyes were watchful. From the way Max had reacted when Bess asked about his scar, Nancy knew she would have to be cautious questioning him.

"Yeah, we're having a good time," Nancy said casually. "And we're getting curious about the rafting business. Are there many rafting companies on Lost River?"

Max picked up a stick and turned it in his fingers. "Maybe a half-dozen or so. Most of them are headquartered up at the Junction."

"Have you and Paula worked together often?" Nancy asked.

"Nope," Max said, shaking his head.

Nancy waited, hoping he would say something else. "We're sort of curious about her company, White Water Rafting," she went on. "The sign on the building looked new. Has she been in business long?"

"I don't think so."

"And the contest," Nancy pressed. "What do you know about the contest?"

"Nothing," Max replied. "Paula just hired me to run the raft for this trip. She didn't even tell me there was a contest. I heard that from one of the kids after I got here. It seemed a little weird to me."

"Weird?"

"Oh, you know—I mean, what was she running a contest *for*, anyway? But what do I know? I'm just a rafter. I don't know anything about the business end." He raised an eyebrow. "You sure are asking a lot of questions."

Nancy shrugged. "Just curious."

"You know, I've got this feeling that I know you," Max said. "Like maybe I've seen your picture somewhere. Have you been on television or something? Are you famous?"

"No, I wouldn't say I'm famous." Nancy decided it wouldn't hurt to tell him who she was. "Actually, I'm a private detective."

"A pretty *famous* private detective," Ned put in proudly. "Internationally famous."

"So maybe you *have* seen her picture," Bess added. "She's been in the newspapers more than once."

"A detective?" Max asked, surprised. "You mean a private eye, like in books and on TV?"

Linda and Ralph wandered over. "A *girl* detective?" Linda asked curiously. At that, Mike and Tod broke away from the fire and joined the others. They listened intently.

"That's right," Nancy said, laughing.

Max gave her a long look, as if he were trying to remember something. "What kind of cases have you worked on?" he asked.

"Oh, all kinds," Nancy said modestly. "Blackmail, sabotage, embezzlement, murder, theft . . . you name it—"

Suddenly Max gave a quick flicker of recognition—and then, just as suddenly, it was as if a shutter had closed down over Max's eyes. He stood up abruptly. "Got to see about a few things," he said. And he walked quickly away.

Bess looked at Nancy anxiously. She got to her feet, too. "I think I'll just make sure Max isn't angry about something."

Nancy watched Bess follow Max as he walked away. Why had he gotten so upset? She could swear that he recognized her—but she couldn't remember meeting him, and he wasn't exactly the kind of person she would forget. Was Max trying to decide whether to tell her something? That was possible—but it was also possible there was something he would go to any lengths to keep her from finding out.

She frowned as Bess caught up with Max a little distance away. She wished that Bess could manage more control over her feelings. It really wasn't a good idea for her to get so involved so quickly.

Linda stepped forward. "Gosh, I've never known a *real* detective," she said with a shy smile.

"Well, I don't know if I count," Nancy said. "I'm a real detective, all right, but I'm on vacation."

"Well, I sure hope we won't need your services," Ralph said cheerfully.

"Okay, everybody," Paula called. "Lunch break's over!"

By the time the rafts were loaded up again, the sun had faded behind a bank of threatening clouds. Mike asked George to trade places with him so he could ride with Tod. Sammy asked Mercedes to trade places with her, probably because she didn't want to be around Ned and Nancy, so Mercedes sat just ahead of Nancy and Ned, with Tod and Mike in the bow together. Secretly, Nancy was glad that Sammy was on the other raft. And she welcomed the chance to talk to Mercedes. But it was difficult to find out anything from her.

"I don't know the first thing about the contest," Mercedes insisted with a nervous glance over her shoulder at Paula. Nancy sensed that Mercedes was afraid of her cousin. "When I heard about the trip, I asked Paula if I could go. That's all." She bit her thumbnail. "I thought it would be fun to get out on the river. I've never been rafting."

"Did you see any advertisements for the contest?" Nancy asked in a low voice. "The others can't remember entering it." Mercedes shrugged and turned away.

Mercedes *was* afraid of her cousin. But why?

The afternoon was uneventful. For the first couple of hours, there was as much drifting as paddling, then Nancy began to notice that the water was moving more rapidly. Her raft was following the other one down a deep, shadowy gorge where the water ran even faster, foaming and curling against the rocks as the channel of the river narrowed and twisted. In the distance Nancy could hear a deeper sound, like faraway drums echoing between the walls of the cliffs.

"What's that?" she asked nervously.

"Dead Man's Falls," Paula replied.

"Do you think we can skip that landmark?" Nancy kidded.

Tod laughed. "The name makes it sound worse than it is," he said. "A couple of guys drowned there last year, but the rafter was at fault. Sloppy handling."

"You don't know that, Tod," Paula said

58

sharply. "Even the best raft-handlers have trouble there in high water, because of the way the rocks line up."

"Is the water high right now?" Ned asked curiously.

Paula shook her head. "Nope. It's only a four-foot drop, anyway. These eighteen-foot rafts are big enough to take it easily when the water's down, the way it is now."

They came around another bend, and at the far end, the riverbed began to step down in a series of small, rough rapids that tossed the raft against rock after rock. Nancy found herself clinging to the side.

"There's the falls!" Tod shouted, pointing. Nancy looked. She could see Max's raft just ahead.

"Okay," Paula shouted. "This'll be just like going down a steep sliding board. Once we're over, the water will suck us down and then force us up again. It'll be like riding a bucking horse, so hang on. Check your life vests to see that they're fastened."

Nancy looked at the other raft. "That idiot!" Nancy gasped, pointing to Bess. "She's not wearing her life vest!"

"She probably didn't think it looked pretty enough," Ned said with a laugh. He sobered quickly. "She's not a very strong swimmer, is she?"

Nancy shook her head, cinching her own life jacket a little tighter. "Sometimes Bess doesn't have much sense," she muttered.

The raft gathered speed as the current dragged it toward the falls. A few yards upstream, Max's raft seemed to hang up against a rock. Frantically, Max fought the current with his oars, and Ralph tried to push off.

"Uh-oh!" Paula muttered. "That's real trouble!"

Nancy and the others watched helplessly as the raft broke loose from the rock and was captured by the swirling water. It somersaulted broadside over the lip of the falls, heaving its shrieking passengers to almost certain death in the raging torrent.

"Bess!" Nancy screamed into the cold spray, hardly feeling it sting her face. "Answer me! Bess! Where are you?"

Chapter

Eight

PAULA LEANED ON the oars. "Hang on!" she shouted. "We're going over!" And with that the raft poised for a nosedive over the edge of the falls.

The bow hit the water at the foot of the falls with an enormous splash that drenched everyone, dived down, and came up again, riding the crest of a wave. Paula dug in deep with the oars, and in a moment they were out of the worst of the swirling current. They were carried fifty yards below the falls before they could beach the raft on a jutting sandbar.

Everybody abandoned the raft and dashed

back upstream. In the gorge, the evening shadows were already falling, but Nancy could see heads bobbing in the frothing water. Linda was clinging desperately to a large rock, Ralph keeping a firm hand around her waist. Max supported Sammy as he swam toward them, towing her. And she could see George's dark head in the water, about twenty feet out, one arm waving frantically. But where was Bess?

"There she is!" Ned shouted as Bess's head emerged from the water. "George has her." He dived into the water.

"Hurry, Ned!" Nancy cried. "She's going down again!"

With powerful strokes, Ned swam toward George and Bess, catching Bess just as she slipped out of George's grasp and disappeared again under the white water. He towed her back to the bank, George just ahead of him.

Nancy and George bent over their friend's limp form as Ned pulled her up on the sand. "Bess! Are you all right?"

Nancy rolled her over on her stomach and lifted her up by the middle. The water emptied out of her. After a minute, Bess spluttered and sat up. "I—I'm okay," she said, shaking the water out of her hair. "What happened?"

"Capsize," Tod said grimly. He had thrown a line to Ralph and Linda, and the two of them were now safely on the bank, holding on to each other. Mike was salvaging some of their gear from the water. Paula and Max had clambered back under the falls to detach the raft from a jagged rock.

Tod turned back to Nancy, scowling darkly. He began to coil the line in his hands. "You saw what happened," he said. "Max let the raft get broadside to the current and dumped everybody. Just like the last time."

"Last time?" Nancy said sharply.

"Yeah, when the two guys drowned."

Bess looked up, her eyes wide. "What are you saying?"

"I'm saying it was Max's fault just like last year's capsize," Tod replied. "Max was the rafter I was talking about earlier. His raft got hung up last year and flipped. Everybody fell out—that's how Max got his scar. Only last year there wasn't another raft standing by, and two people drowned." Tod shook his head angrily and slung the coil of rope over his shoulder. "That's why Mike traded places with George. He wouldn't ride with Max on this part of the trip. Once you lose your nerve at a dangerous spot like this, it's tough to get it back."

"Does Paula know about what happened last year?" Nancy asked, her mind shifting quickly into detective gear.

"Yeah, she knows," Tod said bitterly. "Everybody on the river knows. None of the other rafting companies will hire Max now—she shouldn't have either."

63

"How many other people on *this* trip know?" Nancy asked.

Tod shrugged. "Mike. And Paula. I guess that's it. Why?"

"No reason." Nancy stood up. Could the anonymous caller have known about Max's past—and wanted to warn her? But why had *she* been the one to get the call?

"We've got a problem, gang," Paula announced soberly when she and Max returned. Mike and Tod had built a roaring fire beside the remaining raft, and everybody was gathered around it, trying to dry off. They shivered in the cool evening breeze that funneled up through the gorge.

"A problem?" Ned asked.

"Yeah," Paula replied, shrugging into her roomy red-and-black plaid jacket. "The raft got pretty badly beaten up by the water. It's ripped in a half-dozen places—totally beyond repair."

George stared. "Beyond repair? But that means . . ."

"That means we'll have to load everybody into one raft," Paula said matter-of-factly. "Either that, or we'll have to leave some of you here while the others go downriver and send help back." She paused and looked around. "That's going to be a problem, too, because most of the gear that was in that raft—sleeping bags, tents, food—has all been washed away."

"Ooh!" Linda wailed. "Ralph, I *told* you we shouldn't have come!"

"What I want to know," Sammy demanded sharply, "is how this happened. What about it, Max? How come we capsized?"

Max spread his hands out over the fire for warmth. "I don't know," he said slowly. "There's this V-shaped rock just upstream of the falls, hidden under the water. The raft can't go over it, and somehow, we got hung up on it and the current shifted us broadside to the falls." He shrugged. "You know the rest."

"Yeah, we know," Sammy said in a low voice, poking the fire viciously. "We're lucky to be alive, that's what we know."

Nancy looked at Tod. For a minute she thought he was going to tell the others what he had told her. When he didn't she breathed a little easier. It would only make things more difficult if the others knew about the first accident.

"Listen, I know you're all upset," Paula said. "But you'll feel better in the morning, when you're not so tired." She glanced at the grove of willows behind them. "It's going to get dark before long. I suggest we gather enough firewood to last the night, fix ourselves some supper, and bed down early. Tomorrow morning we can decide what to do."

"I want to decide right now," Sammy said sullenly.

Ralph spoke up. "I think the girls ought to be the ones to go out tomorrow on the raft. The guys can stay behind and wait."

"I don't think that's fair," Tod said. "I think we ought to draw straws to see who goes out."

"But I thought Paula said we could all go in one raft," Bess pointed out.

Ned turned to Paula. "Is that safe? I don't think we would have made it over those falls if we had been loaded any heavier."

Paula looked grim. "I wouldn't really recommend everybody going in one raft," she admitted. "Of course, if we had to, I suppose we could."

"There's another big rapids about three miles downstream," Max said, looking very tired. "I think we'd be asking for trouble if we all tried to go in one raft."

"How about a vote?" Nancy suggested.

When they raised their hands, it was six to four in favor of splitting the group.

"So, that leaves us with the decision of who to keep and who to throw away," Mike joked.

"We can draw straws—or twigs," Sammy said.

It was decided that George, Nancy, Sammy, Mike, and Ralph, would be going downstream in the morning with Max. The others would wait.

"Well, I don't know about the rest of you," Nancy said, "but I'm hungry."

"Food's got *my* vote," Bess said.

"Firewood first, then food," Paula said. "And we'd better check what kind of sleeping gear we have."

An hour later, a huge pile of driftwood was stacked on the beach, a pot of Mercedes's thick stew with dumplings was simmering on the fire, and a stack of peanut-butter-and-jelly sandwiches sat on a plate nearby. A pot of hot chocolate was perched next to the fire on a flat rock. The gear had been pulled out and inspected: there were four sleeping bags and six blankets. Nancy's and Ned's packs were wet, but otherwise unharmed; George's and Bess's had been swept away in the capsize.

"Well, at least we'll sleep with a full stomach," George said, leaning back against a rock, her feet to the fire. "That stew was great, Mercedes."

"Yes, it *was* good," Nancy added.

"Thanks," Mercedes said, sounding preoccupied. She was sitting on the other side of the fire with a surly Sammy. "I'm glad it wasn't Paula's raft that went over," she went on. "At least tonight's supper didn't get dumped."

"What *is* our food situation?" Mike asked.

"We lost what was in Max's raft, of course," Paula said. She and Max were sitting together. From time to time Paula had looked at Nancy intently, and once Max had seemed to be getting very angry. He had looked over at

Nancy at that point too, as if they were talking about *her*. "But we've got enough for one more day, if we're careful. We'll leave most of it with the group that's staying here, since it'll be a day or so before we can get back with another raft."

Tod reached in his pocket for his knife. "We can always go hunting," he said, flipping the knife open and running his thumb down the edge of the shiny blade. "Last year I got a squirrel with this thing."

"I wish you'd keep that knife in your pocket, Tod," Linda said irritably. "It makes me nervous."

"Everything makes you nervous, little lady," Tod teased, leaning toward her.

Ralph put his hand on Tod's shoulder. "Give me the knife," he said softly, "or I'll take it away from you."

"You and who else?" Tod scrambled to his feet.

Without warning, Ralph stepped forward easily, his open hand ramming Tod in the chest. Tod's arms flew up as he tumbled backward. His knife fell at Ralph's feet.

"Just me," Ralph replied pleasantly, picking up the knife. He turned to Mike, who was sitting open-mouthed. "Here. Why don't you keep this for your friend. He's a little careless with it."

"A smooth karate style," Nancy said, staring

admiringly at Ralph. "He reminds me of a certain mild-mannered reporter."

Ned laughed. "Yeah, Clark Kent in disguise."

Tod had picked himself off the ground and was brushing himself off. He snatched his knife out of Mike's hand and glared at Ralph. "Next time," he threatened, "it won't be so easy, hotshot."

"Well, I know what's going to be easy for me," Ned said, yawning. "Sleep."

"Good night, Nancy," he whispered tenderly, bending over to kiss her. "And remember, no matter what happens on this crazy vacation, at least we're together."

"Right," she said softly. "At least we're together."

Nancy, George, and Bess bedded down close to the fire, huddling under blankets. "I'm beginning to wish I'd listened to Bess," George mumbled.

Bess pulled her blanket up over her chin. "I'm glad you didn't. If we'd gone to the beach, I'd never have met Max."

George sat up. "You can still care about that guy after what he did to us today?"

Bess sat up, too. "How do you know that the capsize wasn't an accident!"

"How do you know it *was?*" George asked, folding her arms.

"I wish you guys would go somewhere else to argue," Nancy said.

In the distance, an owl hooted eerily, and Bess dived under the blanket. Nancy and George laughed, and they all fell into a restless sleep.

There was no moon that night. The faint starshine hardly penetrated the deep shadows of the gorge. So, when Nancy awakened to the sound of footsteps crunching stealthily on the gravel, her eyes opened to darkness.

Then, an odd ripping noise and a muttered curse. Had a man spoken—or a woman?

Nancy slipped from between George and Bess, who both were sleeping soundly, and headed for the noise. She'd almost reached the river when she saw a figure—little more than a deeper shadow in the darkness—moving in front of her.

"Who is it?" Nancy asked.

The only answer was a blow to her shoulder as the figure rammed past her, to melt into the night and disappear.

Chapter

Nine

NOISELESSLY, NANCY TRIED to follow, but after a few moments, she had to admit that she had lost whomever it was she had seen and had no choice but to crawl back under the blanket and try to get some sleep.

She was awake as soon as the sun touched the lip of the sheer cliff on the other side of the river. Quietly, trying not to disturb Bess and George, she crept out from under the blanket and pulled on her tennis shoes, which were still damp from the day before.

George stirred reluctantly. "What are you doing up at this hour?" she asked sleepily.

"I heard footsteps last night, and a funny noise," Nancy replied, tugging a comb through her tangled hair. "I'm going to look around and see what I can find."

"I'll come with you," George offered, throwing off the blanket. She had slept in the jeans and sweatshirt she had put on after the dunking, but she was still shivering. "It's *cold!*" she exclaimed, rummaging in her duffel bag for her red jacket.

The ashes of the previous night's campfire still glowed in the chilly gray dawn. Beyond, the raft was like the shadowy carcass of a beached whale.

"That's odd," Nancy said, staring. "Doesn't the raft look a little lopsided?"

Nancy and George ran forward, then stopped, gasping in horror. The raft had been slashed from end to end, and its rubber walls were soft and deflated. Even though she didn't know much about rafts, Nancy could tell that the rips were much too large to be repaired.

"Well, *this* was no accident," George said grimly. "Somebody wants to keep us from getting out of here."

"That must have been the noise I heard last night!" Nancy said.

"Remember Tod's threat to get even with Ralph?" George said thoughtfully. "Do you suppose this is how he tried to do it?"

"Boy, you guys sure are up early," Ned said groggily. He appeared behind them, rubbing the sleep out of his eyes and shivering in spite of his heavy down vest. "I hope you were warmer last night than I—" His eyes widened as he saw the damaged raft. He whistled softly between his teeth. "Uh-oh! Now we're *really* up a creek."

"I'll say," Nancy agreed crossly. "And I wish you wouldn't make such awful puns so early in the morning."

"Sorry," Ned said. "But who do you think did it? More important, what do we do *now?*"

Nancy shrugged. She told him what she had heard the night before. "I got up to investigate, but whoever it was made off into the dark before I could catch him."

"Or her," George added. "You said that the voice you heard might have been a woman's." She shook her head distractedly. "I can't imagine why anybody would do this. I mean, we're all in this mess together, aren't we? Whoever did it is just as stuck as we are."

"Right," Nancy replied. She got down on her hands and knees and examined the damp sand. It was packed hard, and she couldn't see any footprints. Carefully, she went over the entire raft, looking for clues. "Dead end," she concluded, staring at the disabled raft. "Well, I guess Ned's right. We've got a bigger question than 'Who?' It's 'Now what?' I'm afraid we're down to a matter of survival.''

"Who would do such a thing?" Sammy cried angrily a short while later as the group stood looking at the raft. Gradually the horrible truth dawned on her. "Hey, it's got to be one of *us!* One of *us* did this—and whoever it is, he's got to be crazy!"

"Tod's the one with the knife!" Linda said shrilly. "Remember what he said last night about getting even? And look! He's wearing a bandage. I'll bet he cut himself last night when he was cutting up the raft!"

Tod shook his head violently. "You're not pinning this thing on *me,*" he protested.

"How did you cut your hand?" Nancy asked him calmly.

Tod looked at the ground. "Mike and I were having a little game of knife-throwing—after everyone went to sleep," he said. "And I—I just got careless, that's all."

"He's right," Mike spoke up quickly. "It happened the way he said. I saw it."

"Yeah, how do we know you're not just covering up for your friend?" Ralph asked, stepping forward, his fists clenched.

Tod stepped backward, away from Ralph. He licked his lips nervously. "Why would *I* want to hole the raft?" he said. "I've got to get out of here just like everybody else, don't I?" He jerked his finger toward Max. "If you want to know what *I* think, I think *he* did it. He finished off one raft yesterday afternoon under the falls, and he got the other one last night."

"Hey!" Max said angrily. "You've got no right—"

"Yeah, well, you're the guy with the bad record," Mike put in.

"Bad record?" Sammy asked.

"That's right," Tod replied. "Yesterday's 'accident' at the falls wasn't the first time Max has been in trouble. He's responsible for the drownings of two men here last year."

"Yesterday *was* an accident!" Bess exclaimed heatedly as everybody stared, horror-stricken, at Max. "Anyway, whatever happened last summer doesn't have anything to do with last night. Why would *Max* want to sabotage the raft?"

"Why would *anybody* want to sabotage the raft?" Mercedes asked quietly. Nancy noticed that her face was very pale, and that her voice sounded flat and hard, as if she were trying to keep it steady.

"Only somebody who's a little crazy," Linda answered, her voice going high with terror. She turned to Nancy. "You're a detective. Can you make any sense out of this?"

"Not so far," Nancy replied. She looked

around the group. "Did anybody see or hear anything out of the ordinary during the night?"

All the heads shook negatively. "Well, then, did anybody see anyone get up in the middle of the night?" More head shaking. "One more question. Who were you sleeping close to?"

"Well, the four of us were sleeping together," George volunteered. "You, me, Bess under the blanket, and Ned in his sleeping bag."

"And Linda and I slept side by side," Ralph said. Linda blushed.

"I slept next to Tod," Mike volunteered. "And I can guarantee that he didn't get up."

"Right," Sammy muttered. "And I'll bet he says the same for you."

"How about you, Sammy?" Nancy asked.

"I slept next to Mercedes, if you have to know," Sammy said loftily. "And Paula slept on the other side of me."

Nancy turned to Max. "That leaves you, Max," she said.

"Yeah, I know where that leaves me," he replied bitterly. "Under suspicion. I slept by myself."

"Actually, *everybody's* under suspicion," Nancy said, turning back to the group. "Any of us could have gotten up without the others knowing. I'm proof of that."

Paula stepped forward. "Well, now that our internationally famous detective has struck out, we've got some important decisions to make," she said.

Nancy looked closely at Paula. She looked almost satisfied.

"Yeah," Sammy said. "What *do* we do? Do we hike out downriver?"

"No way," Max answered firmly. "This gorge goes on for three or four miles with no banks. There's no way we can walk along the edge of the river."

Ned looked up the cliff wall. At first it had seemed almost vertical, stretching fifty feet or more straight toward the sky, but he could see places for footholds. "It looks like a tough climb out that way," he said, "but we might be able to make it."

"I don't know . . ." Paula said.

Nancy brightened. "Wait a minute. We've got a radio. Right?"

"Right," Paula answered slowly.

"Then why don't we radio for help? In fact," Nancy asked, looking questioningly at Paula, "why didn't we radio yesterday after the accident?"

"Because," Paula said almost too quickly. "You—that is I—didn't think the signal would reach that far." Her amber eyes blazed at Nancy. "Are you satisfied?"

Nancy wasn't sure, Paula looked so flustered.

"Hey, I'm almost positive the signal would

reach," Mike put in confidently. "It broadcasts through the repeater tower at the ranger station."

"Yeah," Max said, "the tower would boost the signal so that it could be received at ranger headquarters."

"Then if we send them a message, they'll come to rescue us?" Linda asked hopefully.

"That's right," Mike said, and he and Max suddenly looked sheepish.

"I don't know what's wrong with me," Max grumbled. "With everything going on, I didn't think of the most obvious thing." His face reddened. "I forgot we even *had* a radio."

"Me, too," Mike admitted. "The way my mind's been working the past day or so, I was thinking it got dumped when the first raft flipped."

"Where *is* the radio?" Bess asked.

Max reached under the platform on the raft. "Right here," he said, pulling out a small, waterproof box.

The radio was a small, hand-held model with a pull-out antenna, almost like a walkie-talkie. Max flipped on the power switch. Nancy, watching closely, saw his mouth tighten. He flipped the switch again.

"What's wrong?" she asked.

Max shook his head impatiently. "I don't know," he said, clicking the switch on and off, "but the power won't go on."

"Ohhh," Bess and Linda chorused nervously.

Max raised his shoulders, heaving a sigh. "Well, Ned, I guess your direction is the one we take."

"Direction?" Ned said quizzically. "What direction?"

"Up," Max said grimly, eyeing the steep cliff face. "Straight up."

Chapter

Ten

PAULA GRABBED THE radio away from Max. "What do you mean, it's not working? Didn't you check the batteries before we left?"

For a moment, Max looked confused. "Yeah," he mumbled. "I even put new ones in. The radio was working just fine."

Paula fiddled with the power switch. "Well, it's not working now," she said disgustedly. "Great. That's all we need, to be stranded out here without an operating radio."

"Here, let *me* see," Mike said, reaching for it. He took the batteries out and then put them back in again—that didn't help. Then he took the back off.

"Check the crystal," Nancy said suddenly.

Mike looked up. "You know something about radios?"

"Not much," she admitted. "But I had a case once where a crystal was stolen from a radio. Does this one need a crystal?"

"A tiny one," Mike said. Intently, he bent over the radio. "Hey! The crystal's gone!"

Linda pointed at Max. "You were the one who put the radio in the raft," she said accusingly. "I *saw* you. You were the last one to touch it. *You* must have taken the crystal!"

"You have no right to make accusations like that," Bess retorted. "The person who sabotaged the raft could just as easily have removed the crystal. Right, Nancy?"

Nancy nodded. "Actually, it could have been taken at any time." She examined the radio case. Even if she had brought her fingerprint kit along, it would have been a hopeless job. The case was made of a roughly grained vinyl that wouldn't hold a print. And there didn't seem to be any other clues.

Mike closed up the radio again. "Well, that's that," he said.

Nancy looked at him. Whoever had done this had to know what the crystal was and where to look for it. Maybe Mike had destroyed the radio and Tod had destroyed the raft—all as part of some silly prank.

She shook her head. Surely not. But the

whole thing was beginning to seem like a hopeless muddle.

Paula glanced at Nancy. "I don't suppose our girl detective has any ideas about who did it," she remarked sarcastically.

Nancy shook her head. "Afraid not," she replied. Then she noticed that Max was staring at Paula, dumbfounded, as if he had suddenly thought of something but wasn't quite sure whether he ought to believe it.

"So?" Sammy demanded. "Do we just sit here and wait for somebody to raft downriver and spot us?"

"I don't think anybody will be coming down until the middle of next week," Paula said. "I checked the schedule board yesterday, just before we left. The next trip downriver doesn't leave until a week from Wednesday."

"By that time we could starve to death!" Linda exclaimed.

"Well, we *have* got another alternative," Paula said.

Everybody looked at her. "What's that?" George asked.

Paula pointed to the top of the cliff. "We can hike out," she replied. "It's a tough climb, as Ned said, but we *could* make it. Once we get to the top, there's a trail, maybe five or six miles back in the woods, that leads to the ranger station, which is another eight or nine miles away. I think I could find the trail."

"Yes, but that means a fourteen-mile hike!" Sammy exclaimed. She looked at Max. "What do *you* think?"

Max gave an uncertain shrug. "I'm a good woodsman, but I don't know anything about the trails in this particular area. We'll have to rely on Paula."

Paula's amber eyes were narrowed to slits. "Maybe some of you don't want to rely on me," she said, turning to Nancy. "You're not afraid of a little walking, are you, Nancy?"

Nancy caught the unpleasant undertone, but answered quietly, "No, I'm not afraid of walking—as long as we're sure of where we're going. At least on the river, we know where we are. Once we're in the wilderness, we could get lost pretty easily." She sneaked a glance at Max, who was still staring at Paula.

"Well, I can't guarantee anything," Paula said crossly. "But I don't see that we've got any alternative."

"Well, then," Ned spoke up quickly, "maybe we ought to take an inventory and figure out how much food we've got. How long will this hike take us?"

"We'll probably get to the ranger station late tomorrow," Paula said.

"And we've got only enough food for today?" Ned asked.

"Looks like we'll be going on half-rations," George said glumly.

"Yes, but that means we won't have to carry so much," Paula pointed out. "Just our sleeping gear and whatever jackets and sweaters you have. It's going to get pretty cold up there tonight." She looked around. "Ned, will you and Max inventory the food and distribute it among the packs so that we all have an equal load to carry? Max!"

"Huh?" Max seemed to be jerked away from his thoughts. "What did you say?"

Paula put her hands on her hips. "If you'd been listening," she said, "you'd know. I asked you and Ned to inventory the food. Mercedes, there's a tarp in the raft. Better get it out—Tod will give you a hand. The tarp might come in handy if it rains tonight. Ralph, get the flashlight and the lantern." She fished in her pocket. "Bess?"

"Yes?"

"Here's a compass. I'm giving you the job of checking our direction so we don't end up wandering in circles. When we get to the top of the cliff, I'll show you how to read it. Okay?"

"Well, okay," Bess said. "I mean, I'm not very good at things like that, but—"

"You'll do fine," Paula said shortly. She picked up her red-and-black plaid jacket and slung it over her shoulder. "Okay, everybody. Let's break camp! Take what you need to keep warm and dry, but don't take anything that you don't want to carry for the next two days!"

The cliff wasn't quite as steep as it had looked from below. Bushes and small trees grew in the rocky rubble, and the hikers found plenty of hand- and footholds.

"I want you to climb in front of me, Nancy," Ned said as they got ready. "That way, if you slip, I'm right behind you."

The climb took the group almost two hours. The rocks were soft and crumbling from exposure to the weather, and Nancy had to concentrate on where she put her feet. Above her, Bess and George moved up carefully, pressing close to the steep slope. Nobody said much.

They were almost at the top when Nancy heard a scream from below, then the sound of loose rock sliding and the babble of frantic voices.

"What's happening?" Nancy called to Ned.

"I think it's Linda," he said anxiously, peering down. He pulled a coil of rope from his shoulder. "Hey, down there! Do you need a hand?"

It took three of them—Ralph, Max, and Ned—to hoist Linda to the top. The others were there already, sprawled on the rocky ground, breathless and weary from the climb.

"She's going to be all right. It's only a sprain," Paula said brusquely, probing Linda's ankle with her fingers. "Too bad we don't have any ice for it."

"It hurts," Linda moaned. "I don't think I can walk."

"You'll be okay," Ralph comforted her. "I'll help you."

Ned came out of the woods with a long branch. "We can make a crutch out of this," he said.

After a few minutes, Linda's crutch was ready and the group started out, following Paula. Bess, with the compass, was right behind her.

"We're going northeast," Paula told them, before they started. "Since there's no trail, and the terrain is so rough, we'll be moving slowly. We don't want anybody getting lost."

Nancy nodded, and she and the others set out through the woods. At every step, huge swarms of mosquitoes flew up, and Nancy had to keep swatting them. The sweat poured off her face in little rivers.

"Some vacation," George grunted as she pushed up a vine and tried to crawl under it. "I'll have to call our travel agent when we get home. I think we got into the wrong contest."

"Either that," Nancy said, half chuckling, "or we won the wrong prize."

George swallowed a giggle. "Do you suppose Paula knows where's she's going?" she asked, peering through the tangle of underbrush. "I'd hate to walk through this stuff *twice.*"

"Hey!" Ned kidded. "How can you doubt her? After all, she's got Bess right beside her, carrying our one and only compass."

"That's exactly what I'm worried about," George said.

It was nearly noon by the time they stopped for lunch in a large clearing. The sun filtered through the dense trees, and Bess took off her jacket and tossed it on a nearby rock. She was eating a sandwich, her knees pulled up wearily, her back to a tree, when Nancy sat down beside her.

"Tired?" Nancy asked, taking a bite of her own sandwich. It was the last of the peanut butter, and there was only enough bread for one more meal.

"You know it." Bess sighed. "Paula's in good shape, and keeping up with her in these woods is tough."

"I don't suppose you've found out anything about her," Nancy said, lowering her voice and looking around to be sure she wasn't overheard.

Bess shook her head. "I've tried talking to her, but she won't say a word. I did notice Max watching her in a funny way, though. It's as if he knows something about her that the rest of us don't."

"Yeah, I noticed that, too," Nancy said. She finished her sandwich and stood up, brushing herself off. "And maybe now is a good time to ask him about it." But everybody else was finishing lunch, too, and Nancy didn't have a chance.

"Will you get the compass?" Paula asked Bess just then. "I want to check our direction before we get started again."

"Sure," Bess said, reaching for her jacket, which was spread out on the rock. She felt in the pocket. Then her face went white. Frantically she began to search the other pockets as well.

"What's wrong?" Paula snapped. "Where's the compass?"

"I don't know!" Bess exclaimed, sitting down limply on the rock. "It's not in my pocket and I know it was there before lunch. The compass is gone—now we'll never find our way out of here!"

Chapter

Eleven

"GONE?" GEORGE GASPED. "You lost the compass? I can't believe it. Bess Marvin, you are so *incredibly* careless."

"But I *wasn't* careless!" Bess wailed, holding her jacket like a shield against her. "It *was* here. Somebody must have taken it!"

Nancy glanced at the others. Mike, Tod, and Ralph, were staring at Bess, grim faced. It was obvious that they agreed with George: Bess had lost the compass. Sammy, Linda, and Mercedes had their arms around one another, and Linda was sobbing. They seemed to think that George was right, too. But Max was watching Paula, and he wore the same odd look on his face that Nancy had seen earlier.

What was just as interesting was that Paula seemed to be aware of his gaze. She kept her head turned away from him, and her cheeks were flushed.

She looked darkly at Bess. "Without that compass, I don't know if we *will* find the trail," she said. "These woods are really confusing. We could walk around in circles for a week!"

"What's going to happen?" Sammy whispered. "Are we going to *die* here?"

"Nancy Drew is supposed to be the expert in finding things out," Paula said. "Why don't you ask her?"

"Wait a minute!" George shouted. "Nancy doesn't know anything about the woods. *You're* supposed to be *that* expert!"

"Yeah, well, you can't expect me to be much of an expert without a compass," Paula growled.

"Nancy, I have to talk to you," Ned said quietly, coming up behind her. He pulled her into the woods. "Bess didn't lose the compass," he said when they were out of earshot. "I saw who took it!"

Nancy waited expectantly.

"It was *Paula*," said Ned, mystified. "She waited until she thought nobody was watching, and she took it out of Bess's pocket."

"Paula!" Nancy exclaimed. "Why would she do that?"

Ned shook his head. "I don't know. But I wasn't the only one who saw her take it. Max did, too. And it was funny: *I* was surprised, but I don't think Max was. I think he half suspected that Paula might try something."

"I saw him give her a strange look this morning, after we discovered the raft. Maybe he suspected then that she had wrecked it. I think he's been keeping an eye on her all day."

Ned's face was tight. "Well, if that's what he's been doing, Paula knows," he said. "She looked up and saw him watching her take the compass."

"That *really* complicates things," Nancy said.

Ned frowned. "Do you think Paula could have destroyed the raft?"

"It's possible, although for the life of me I can't think of a motive. I can't think of a motive for her taking the compass, either. But I'm still disturbed by it—the broken radio, too. Right now, though, I want to find out what *Max* thinks."

"Are you going to question him?"

Nancy hesitated. "I was going to. But instead, maybe we should keep our eye on the two of them for a while. We might learn more." She laughed a little. "At least we're not as lost as Paula wants us to think we are."

Ned put his arms around Nancy's shoulders. "Listen, Nan," he said, turning her toward him as they walked back to face the group. "We're in a tight spot right now, but whatever happens," he went on, his voice getting tight, "I want you to know how much I love you."

Nancy felt her arms go around his neck. "I love you, too, Ned," she whispered, letting herself forget Paula, forget the river, forget everything but the kiss Ned bent down to give her.

"Nancy!" It was Bess calling. "Nancy, where are you?" Bess appeared behind Nancy and Ned, George right behind her.

"Here I am." Reluctantly Nancy broke away from Ned's arms.

"Nancy, you've got to get George off my back," Bess begged, tears streaking down her dusty face.

"Get off your back?" George exploded. "The way I feel right now I'll be on your back for thirty-five years—if we live that long." George spun Bess around. "I've put up with lost car keys, lost plane tickets, even lost money—but this thing, Bess Marvin . . ."

"Knock it off!" Nancy held her hand up. She turned to George. "Bess didn't lose the compass. Ned saw Paula take it out of Bess's pocket."

George's eyes grew round. "Paula!" she exclaimed.

Bess stared at Nancy, consternation on her face. "Why would Paula do that? Is she *trying* to get us lost?"

"It's beginning to look that way," Nancy admitted. "Max saw her steal the compass, too, and I think he also suspects her of holing the raft."

George put her arms around Bess. "I'm sorry I blew up at you," she said. "Really."

"It's okay, George," Bess replied, patting her cousin on the shoulder. "Everybody is uptight right now. We're in a real mess."

"Bess is right," Ned said soberly. "Some of those kids—Linda and Sammy especially—look as if they might go to pieces at any minute. If George can blow up this way, others are bound to."

"That's what worries me," Nancy said. "We can't tell the others just yet about Paula taking the compass, so they're going to continue to accuse Bess." She turned to her friend. "Can you stick it out for a little while?"

Bess smiled weakly. "As long as I know you guys believe me."

"George, it might be a good idea if you continued to act angry at Bess," Nancy said. "That'll keep Paula from getting suspicious."

"My pleasure," George teased. She gave Bess a friendly poke.

"George!" Bess responded, trying not to laugh.

When Nancy and her friends rejoined the group, they found them quarreling about which direction to take. Nancy could see that the group spirit was beginning to deteriorate rapidly.

"This is all your fault," Sammy told Bess bitterly as they began to make their way through the woods again. "We're all going to *die* in this wilderness, and *you're* responsible!"

"Sammy's right," George agreed, playing her part. "If you hadn't lost the compass, at least we would know which direction we were heading in!"

Looking unhappy, Bess didn't answer.

Except for the occasional angry quarrels that seemed to break out with greater frequency, the group walked in silence for the next two hours. The terrain became even rougher as they moved away from the river. Walking was very difficult, especially for Linda, who was limping along with her crutch, leaning heavily on Ralph and moaning every few minutes.

Nancy walked within hearing distance of Max and Paula, keeping a careful eye on them.

Suddenly she was aware of the noise of tumbling water. "What's that?" she asked, catching up to Max and Paula. "Is it Lost River? Are we going in circles?"

"I don't think so," Paula said. She had tied the sleeves of her jacket around her waist, but now she pulled the jacket on. "If I'm right," she continued, "that's Little Horn Creek. The trail isn't too far away."

Little Horn Creek was in a deep ravine, full of rocks and tangled trees. The group, which was nearly exhausted, stopped to rest on a rocky ledge, partway up the cliff over the ravine.

"Thank goodness," Sammy said with a sigh, sinking down against the rock. "I can't walk another step."

"You've got to," Tod told her. "It's either that or stay here and starve to death—or die of exposure."

Sammy burst into tears. "Stop saying that! You're just trying to scare me!"

"No," Mike said quietly, "it's the truth."

Max seemed to have made up his mind about something. He looked up at the cliff and then at Paula. "The cliff top looks clear," he said. "The climb is a little rough, Paula, but I think you and I can make it. Let's climb up there and see if we can tell where we are."

Paula considered his suggestion. "Good idea," she said, after a moment. She raised her voice. "The rest of you stay here and rest. Max and I are going to climb to the top. We'll be back in a few minutes." The two of them began to scale the cliff, which rose up vertically behind the ledge.

"I wish we could climb up there and hear what they say," Nancy said fretfully, watching them climb the sheer wall.

"No way, Drew," Ned said, coming up behind her. "Climbing that rock is a job for experts. I have the feeling that Max picked the top of the cliff to talk to Paula because he knew we couldn't follow up there, and he didn't want any uninvited listeners." He pulled Nancy down beside him. "Come on, relax. There's nothing we can do but wait."

They waited. In about fifteen minutes, Nancy began to stir worriedly. At that moment, she heard Paula's voice, although the words were indistinguishable. A few small rocks showered down the cliff ten yards to their right. Then there was the sound of a violent scuffle and a loud, dull thump. "No, Max!" Paula cried clearly. Nancy could hear terror in her voice. "Don't!"

"Max! Paula!" Ned shouted, looking up.

For a minute or two there was silence. Then, in a flash of red and black, a limp body hurtled spread-eagled through the air and down into the depths of the creek!

Chapter
Twelve

THAT WAS PAULA!" Linda screamed.

Mercedes moaned and turned away, covering her eyes. Ashen-faced, Sammy put her arms comfortingly around her.

"Do you think she's dead?" Tod asked, peering over the edge. "Can you see her? Where is she?"

"There," Mike said excitedly, pointing down the ravine. "In the creek." They all watched in incredulous horror as Paula's plaid jacket ballooned up in the deep water of the creek far below, buoying the body along almost like a life jacket. It drifted lazily in the water for a minute

97

or two, then it was sucked into the swift current and swept down over a jumble of rocks and out of sight.

"We've got to get down there!" Mercedes said, struggling hysterically against Sammy's restraining arms.

Ned shook his head. "It's a fifty-foot cliff," he said. "None of us has the experience to climb it, especially without any rock-climbing gear. Anyway, the chances of survival from a fall like that are next to nothing." He gave Mercedes a sympathetic look. "We'll have to send a team back to recover her body—after *we* get out."

"Max!" Bess suddenly exclaimed. She looked up the cliff. "Where *is* he?"

Tod laughed harshly. "If you were Max, would you hang around to shake hands with your audience after you'd murdered somebody?"

"Murdered?" Linda whispered, her mouth dropping open. "You mean Max pushed her?"

"Wait a second. We don't know that Max—" Bess began hesitantly.

George whipped around to confront her. "For Pete's sake, Bess. We heard their fight. We heard Paula scream. And then we saw her go over. It's as simple as one, two, three. Paula's dead and Max killed her!"

Bess sat down and put her face in her hands.

"I'm afraid George may be right, Bess,"

Nancy said gently, kneeling beside her. "But there is still a chance Max may not have killed Paula. After all, we don't know exactly what happened up there—only what we saw and heard."

"What do you want? A signed confession?" Tod said.

"But why?" asked Ralph. "Did he and Paula sabotage both rafts and the radio just to get us stranded out here?" He shook his head in puzzlement. "It doesn't make sense."

"Maybe Paula found out that Max did all those things," Tod suggested. "And when she confronted him with what she knew, he pushed her over the edge to shut her up."

"Could be," Mike said. "Or maybe she was getting on his case about capsizing the raft. Between that and those drownings last year, he'd be finished on the river. Maybe she said something—"

"Listen, everybody," Nancy broke in. "Before you get too far out on a limb with your theories, I'd better tell you that Paula stole the compass out of Bess's pocket. Ned saw her take it—and so did Max."

"*Paula* took it?" Mercedes exclaimed. "Why?" It seemed to Nancy that there was an odd note in her voice, almost as if *Mercedes* had half suspected that that might happen.

Nancy nodded, convinced Mercedes knew

more than she was revealing. Maybe with Paula out of the picture, Mercedes would be willing to talk.

"I think Max believed Paula holed the raft, as well," Nancy continued, "and that he thought he knew what her motive was. I intended to question him about it this afternoon, but now it's too late."

"But *why?*" Sammy demanded. "Ralph's right. It just doesn't make sense. Why would Paula take the compass?"

"Maybe she wanted to keep us lost, for some reason we don't understand," Ned pointed out. "Don't forget, as long as *she* had the compass, *she* wasn't lost. She could find her way out—even if the rest of us couldn't."

"So you're suggesting that *Paula* was up to something," George said thoughtfully.

Nancy nodded. "Yes, but we probably won't know what until we can talk to Max. That's why it's so important that we find him."

Sammy shivered. "Well, *you* can have the pleasure of finding him. If *I* saw him, I'd run as fast as I could in the other direction. He's dangerous!"

"Right now," Nancy said, "we have to concentrate on finding our way out of here. Then we have to find Max—dangerous or not."

They sat for a few more minutes on the ledge, trying to decide which direction they should take.

"Paula seemed to be headed up this creek," Ned pointed out, picking up his pack and adjusting it over his shoulders. "I think we should keep on in that direction. Tod, you and Mike are the ones who are most at home in the woods. I vote that you try to pick out the trail for us."

They set off again with their packs, even more subdued this time, following Tod and Mike. The going got steeper and steeper, and the underbrush seemed to grow more dense with every yard. Just as Nancy had decided that she was too exhausted to climb over one more twig, the terrain flattened out and the forest opened up. Ahead was the dim outline of what looked like an old logging road, leading in both directions into the dense woods.

"Finally," Linda moaned, sitting down in the middle of the trail.

"What luck!" Sammy said, dropping her pack wearily. "I was beginning to think we'd *never* find it!"

"This isn't luck," Tod said, grinning. "It's superior woodsmanship!"

"Whatever it is," Nancy said, "I'm grateful. Which way is the ranger station?" she asked Mike. "Right or left?"

Mike looked blank. "You've got me," he said.

"Do *you* know?" Nancy asked Tod.

Tod frowned. "Not for sure. But I'd say it's

probably that way." He jerked his thumb to the right.

"What makes you say that?" Mike asked quickly. "If I had to guess, I'd say it's probably *that* way." He pointed to the left. "Once I saw the ranger station on a map, and I think it's farther south than this."

"But the ranger station has a fire tower," Tod argued. "They always build fire towers high up. And the trail to the right goes *up*."

"I think you're dead wrong," Mike said flatly.

"Hey, you guys," Ned said. "We've got to make a decision."

"We could split up," Ralph suggested tentatively. "Whichever group reaches the ranger station could get help for the others."

"No way!" Sammy said. "With ten of us, we're a big enough group to handle most situations. A smaller group might get into trouble."

Ned nodded vigorously. "I agree. There's safety in numbers."

"Let's vote," George said. "I vote for going uphill."

Nancy counted hands. The majority wanted to go to the right.

"I just don't think I can walk uphill anymore," Linda said, beginning to cry again.

"We don't have any choice," Ralph said, helping her up. "Come on. The sooner we get going, the sooner we'll be there."

"Well, we can't count on getting there today," Ned reminded them.

"You mean we've got to spend the night in the woods?" Linda asked.

"I mean that Paula told us that the ranger station was seven or eight miles away, once we got on the fire trail," Ned said. "That's a good five-hour hike, at the rate we're going. And it's going to get dark soon. We need to think about finding somewhere to camp."

"Okay, everybody," Tod said. "Let's start keeping our eyes open for a campsite." He shook their only canteen. "And a spring, too. We're almost out of water."

"Out of water?" Mercedes asked faintly. "What about the food?"

Ned shook his head. "We've got some beef jerky and some dried fruit left," he said. "And three packages of instant soup. In other words, there's enough for supper and maybe breakfast, if we're willing to go on short rations tonight." He frowned. "Let's hope we find some ripe berries."

"Remember what happened the last time we found ripe berries," Bess reminded him.

The group gathered themselves together and set out along the trail.

Before long the sun began to drop toward the western horizon. In places, the trail was littered with rocks—some of them very large—and everyone had to pick their way gingerly across

103

the unstable ground, trying not to trigger rock slides.

Nancy was walking a few paces ahead of Ned when suddenly she felt a peculiar prickle between her shoulder blades. She turned around, but there was only Ned behind her. He grinned wearily.

"Everything okay?" he asked. "You've been pulling farther and farther behind."

Nancy wiped the sweat from her face. "I may be crazy, but I think we're being watched—and I want to watch back."

"That's funny. I've been thinking the same thing."

Nancy paused, listening. "Ned!" she exclaimed, looking up. "Someone's—"

Her voice was drowned out by a loud crash, and a rumble that seemed to shake the earth. Nancy stood frozen. A huge boulder had broken loose from its place on the hillside above. It was hurtling straight at her!

Chapter

Thirteen

NANCY! LOOK OUT!" Ned shouted. He lunged at her, grabbing her arm and pulling her out of the path of the careening boulder. Nancy could feel the huge rock rumbling the earth beneath her feet as it thundered down the hill. When it reached the bottom, it tore like an out-of-control truck into two pines, splintering them at the base, before it rolled to a shuddering halt in a spruce thicket.

As Ned put his arms around her, Nancy began to tremble uncontrollably. Ned's arms felt so strong and protective, as if they could shield her from anything the world could throw at her. She leaned against him, gazing up the hill, and caught a glimpse of shadowy movement, something darting into the trees. Was it an animal she had seen—or a human?

Suddenly she realized the enormity of what had just happened. If it hadn't been for Ned's quick action, she'd be smashed like those trees. She swayed dizzily and sagged against Ned.

He held her tightly, then lowered her gently onto a rock.

After a few minutes, Nancy pushed her hair out of her eyes. "I'm okay," she said shakily. Then she laughed. "Lucky we let everyone go on ahead. At least they didn't see me playing handball with that boulder."

Ned grinned for a moment, tracing his finger along her cheek. But as he helped Nancy to her feet, he looked down at her, soberly. "I was scared, Nancy," he said hoarsely. "You could have been killed!"

"Ned," Nancy said, "I saw something moving up there, after the boulder came down. Do you suppose . . ."

". . . that it was Max?"

Nancy nodded.

"I didn't see what you saw, Nan, but it's entirely possible."

"Max might not have intended to kill Paula, but she's dead. Now he's got to worry about us. If we get out of here alive, he knows we'll go straight to the police!"

"So he's got to kill us?" Ned asked.

"If he's guilty," Nancy answered. "Or he might try to scare us so thoroughly that we keep our mouths shut." Nancy shuddered. "Hey," she said, "will you lend me your jacket for a little while? Thinking about Max out there loose gives me the chills."

Ned wrapped his jacket around her. "We've got to let the others know what happened," he said. "Otherwise I'd keep you warm myself."

Nancy grinned at him. "Control yourself, Nickerson—for the time being anyway," she whispered.

The rest of the group had already chosen a camping spot for the night and had divided up the responsibilities for getting settled.

Mercedes was bent over the fire, her cheeks flushed with the heat. She was stirring soup in a small aluminum pan, balanced carefully on three rocks.

Nancy sat down beside her. "Mmm, that smells good," she said appreciatively. "Vegetable?"

Mercedes nodded. "I wish we had more. I'm afraid this is just going to be enough to whet everyone's appetite."

"Well, maybe we'll get lucky tomorrow and find a berry patch," Nancy replied, laughing. "Minus the bear. Or a creek—then maybe we could catch some fish or something."

Mercedes laughed a little, too. "This *has*

been some trip, hasn't it?" she said gravely. She shivered. "I can't believe what happened to Paula. When I get home, I'm going to have to tell her family . . ."

Nancy nodded sympathetically. Then, choosing her words carefully, she said, "Earlier, I asked if you knew about the contest. I was wondering if you remembered anything else about it."

Mercedes shook her head. "I *told* you," she said impatiently. "I don't know a thing. The contest was already set up when I first heard about the trip."

"Well, then, maybe you can tell me something about Paula's business," Nancy went on, "or about her friendship with Max."

Mercedes frowned. "I don't think they were friends at all. Max was just somebody who was available for this trip. Somebody who knew the river."

"Okay, what about her family?" Nancy asked. "Did your families see each other very often?"

Mercedes looked away. "Why do you want to know? There's no point in dragging up the past."

"What past?" Nancy asked sharply.

Mercedes looked flustered. "I—I just meant the things that have happened in the past two days," she said. "We've got to get out of here.

What's the point in trying to figure out why things happened the way they did? Especially now that—" She choked. "Now that Paula is dead." Her eyes filled with tears and she turned back to the fire.

"You might be right. But why," Nancy persisted, "weren't you surprised to learn that Paula had taken the compass? Why did you suspect her?" Nancy knew that if Mercedes would open up, she'd have the key to the case.

"I don't want to talk anymore," Mercedes said sullenly. "You can't *make* me talk to you."

"No," Nancy admitted. "But when we get back to civilization, the police can."

"I'll cross that bridge when I come to it," Mercedes said, removing the pot from the fire and standing up. "Who knows? We might not even get back to civilization. We've still got another day to go, at least." She turned away from Nancy. "Okay, everybody," she called, "the soup's ready."

While Nancy was eating the soup and the piece of beef jerky she had been rationed, she thought about what Mercedes had told her: *There's no point in dragging up the past.* Nancy was sure Mercedes *hadn't* meant the events of the last two days. In fact, she was sure Mercedes knew something—something she wasn't telling. Something she wouldn't tell.

Nancy snuggled into Ned's jacket, glad he

109

wasn't cold and she could keep it around her. Then she frowned, thinking more about the case. Sure, there weren't a lot of clues, but she sensed there were a couple of possibilities right under her nose that she was overlooking. Every once in a while they began to form in her mind, then vanished before she had a chance to focus on them.

Well, she thought resolutely, Mercedes couldn't keep her from finding out the truth. Nothing could, not even the frustration she was feeling. Nancy Drew always got to the bottom of things, and she'd get to the bottom of this case, too—if it *killed* her.

When supper was over, everyone huddled wearily around the fire, scratched and sore from their long hike. There wasn't much conversation. It was a moonless night, and outside the circle of firelight, the dark pressed in ominously.

Then in the near distance, the quiet was shattered by an eerie scream.

"What was that?" Linda cried out, clinging to Ralph.

Tod laughed. "Just a mountain lion," he replied.

"But don't worry," Mike said. "A mountain lion won't attack you unless you corner him. He's a whole lot more fond of rabbits and ground squirrels than he is of people."

Sammy shivered. "Well, he can keep his rabbits and his ground squirrels," she said. "I'll settle for a hamburger with fries and onions."

George groaned tragically, rubbing her stomach. *"Please.* Don't talk about real food. You might just as well knock me out—it would be much kinder."

Nancy threw a glance at Ned, who was sitting next to her. Now was the time to tell everyone what had happened before supper that evening. Briefly, she told her story.

"It must have been Max!" Ralph and Linda exclaimed when Nancy had finished.

"Max?" Bess asked, in a half-longing voice.

"Oh, will you stop, Bess," George said impatiently. "Haven't we got enough trouble without—"

"It's trouble, all right," Nancy said. "If Max really is dangerous, he's not going to let us out of here to tell the police what happened."

Bess shook her head stubbornly. "I can't *believe* that."

"You might believe it if you'd been standing on that trail, staring up at that boulder coming down on Nancy," Ned said. "It was as big as a house. And it sounded like a freight train."

Nancy shuddered, remembering how frightened she had been—and how strong and supportive Ned's arms had felt around her when for a minute she had lost her own strength. It was ironic, she thought. She had wanted Ned to come on this trip so that he could feel a little protective about her. Well, he certainly was protecting her.

"Yeah, but you don't *know* that somebody pushed the rock," Bess was insisting. "It might just have come loose. After all, rock slides happen here all the time, even when there's no one around. Anyway," she went on insistently, "you aren't even sure you saw somebody up there. How do you know that it wasn't just your imagination?"

"I don't," Nancy admitted. "Just the same, we can't afford to take any chances. If Max *did* push that boulder down, he's dangerous." She looked around at the group. "We've got to be careful."

"Careful?" Sammy asked, frowning. "And just how do we do that?"

"Well, for one thing," Nancy answered, "we shouldn't go off by ourselves."

"Yeah," Ned said, "and we need to pay attention to what's going on around us, so that Max isn't able to sneak up on us."

"Then it might be a good idea to keep watches tonight," Mike said, stirring the fire.

"Right," Nancy agreed.

"I was afraid of losing sleep tonight," Bess said, making a face, "but I had it figured a little differently. I thought my *hunger* would keep me awake!"

Ned drew the first watch and Nancy the second. "I'll wake you up in an hour," he promised as Nancy crawled under her blanket between Bess and George. He bent over and kissed her.

"Thanks," Nancy said sleepily. "And Ned?"

"Uh-huh?"

"Thanks for being there this afternoon. It feels good to be alive." She smiled. "You know, if we get out of this in one piece, I swear I'll never take another vacation the rest of my life. Detective work is a lot safer!"

Ned laughed and gave her another quick kiss.

In an hour, he awakened her and she took her turn beside the fire. At the end of her hour, she woke Mike, who had the third watch, before going back to sleep. But her dreams were full of gigantic boulders that roared down on her.

Nancy woke at dawn, curled up into a tight ball, cold and stiff. The campfire was out and Ralph, who had the last watch, was drowsing beside it.

No wonder I'm cold, Nancy thought. My blanket slipped down. She tugged on the blanket, but the end of it seemed to be caught on something. A rock? She raised her head to look—and froze.

A huge rattlesnake lay coiled on the blanket. At Nancy's movement, its head came up, staring at Nancy with beady amber eyes.

Chapter

Fourteen

THE RATTLER'S TAIL was buzzing like a swarm of angry bees. What could Nancy do? Even though her feet weren't trapped under it, if she moved a muscle—or if George or Bess turned over—the snake was bound to strike.

"Ned," Nancy whispered urgently. "Ned, wake up!"

Ned stirred sleepily on the other side of the fire. "What?" he mumbled.

"Ned," she said again, in a low voice. "There's a huge snake on the foot of my blanket."

"A snake?" Ned exclaimed, throwing off his blanket. "Stay put, Nancy. Don't move!"

"Don't you move too fast, either," she whispered.

"What's going on?" Ralph sat up beside the cold fire, rubbing his eyes. "Is it Max? Where is he?"

"No, it's a snake," Ned replied softly, pulling on his shoes and signaling for Ralph to stay still.

The snake's head began to weave back and forth and its tongue flicked nervously. Beside Nancy, George mumbled something in her sleep. *Oh, please, George,* Nancy thought, *don't turn over!* Aloud, she said, "Hurry, Ned! I think it's getting ready to strike!" The buzz of the rattles grew louder.

Noiselessly, Ned circled around behind the snake. He bent down, picked up a large flat rock, and raised it high above his head. Just as the snake coiled itself to strike, Ned brought the rock down hard on its head. For a moment the snake twisted and writhed, and then it lay still.

"Oh, Ned," Nancy said.

"What's going on?" George asked, sitting up. "Who's throwing rocks?"

Bess stirred under the blanket and mumbled something.

George stared unbelievingly at the snake that Ned had stretched out across the foot of the blanket. "Nancy, it's a monster! It's big enough to have eaten both of us for breakfast—in one gulp!"

Bess burrowed deeper into the blanket. "A monster?" she quavered. "Not another bear!"

Nancy laughed and yanked the blanket off Bess's head. "No, it's not another bear," she said teasingly, pulling her friend to a sitting position. "It's only a snake. Wake up and see."

"A snake!" Bess covered up her eyes. "I don't *want* to see!" After a minute she peeked between her fingers. "Yikes!" she screeched. "It *is* a snake!"

"Must be about five feet long," Ned said, hoisting the snake up on a stout stick. "And I count seven rattles and a button." He shook his head. "It's a good thing you woke up when you did, Nancy. This snake is packing a lot of venom. It could have killed you, or made you plenty sick."

"It's a good thing you were here to kill it, Ned," George pointed out.

"George is right," Nancy said. She looked up at Ned. "You know, that's twice in two days," she said soberly.

"Twice?" Ned asked.

"Last night you pulled me out of the path of the rock. This morning you killed the snake. That's twice in two days that you've saved my life."

Ned laughed. "Sounds like it's getting to be a habit."

Ned disposed of the snake under a large pile

of rocks while the others got up and began to break camp. They shared the last of the dried fruit and beef jerky for breakfast and then made their way to a huckleberry patch that Mike had found near the spring the night before. They were careful to make lots of noise to ward off any bear that might be breakfasting there. Then they washed off the berry juice, filled their canteens at the spring, and gathered back at the campsite.

They were a ragtag bunch, Nancy thought, surveying the group. Linda's ankle was so badly swollen she could barely hobble, even with the help of Ned's crutch. Sammy's arms were breaking out with long, red streaks of something that looked like poison ivy, and she was scratching ferociously. Mercedes was withdrawn and uncommunicative, and Mike and Tod seemed to have quarreled again about the direction they should be taking.

"How far away is the ranger station?" Sammy asked. "How long will it take us to get there?"

Tod shrugged. "I'd guess we walked two or three miles yesterday, after we found the trail. If Paula estimated right, we've got maybe five or six miles to go."

"*If* we're going in the right direction," Mike said sullenly.

"There's no point in going through all of that again," Ned said sharply. "We agreed that we would go in this direction. Let's give ourselves a break and stop quarreling."

They set out, with Tod and Mike in front, followed by George and Bess, Mercedes, Sammy, Ralph and Linda, and Ned and Nancy. The trail was even more difficult than it had been the night before, a switchback that zig-zagged up a mountain, through dense woods. The underbrush hung over the faint path like a thick green canopy, shutting out most of the sun, and even in the daylight the shadows seemed ominous. The day before, Nancy had developed a blister on her right heel, and it was rapidly getting worse, making walking even more difficult.

"Did you get a chance to talk to Mercedes last night?" Ned asked Nancy, helping her over a fallen log.

"Well, I tried," Nancy said with a sigh. She bent over to adjust her tennis shoe, trying to relieve the pressure on her blister. "I didn't get anywhere. She really clammed up. But she *did* say something interesting. When I asked her about Paula's family, she said she didn't want to drag up the past."

Ned looked at her. "So she *does* know something."

"Right. But whatever it is, she's not going to tell me."

"Do you suppose she'd tell me?"

"I don't know. It's worth a try."

"I might be able to catch her off guard." He grinned. "Or I might be able to use some of that charm that Sammy seemed to enjoy." He ducked the playful punch Nancy threw at him.

"Listen, Ned," Nancy said, "all joking aside, I think it's a good idea. Why don't you try to catch up to her now and see what you can find out?"

"Okay, I will." Ned put his hand on Nancy's shoulder. "But you've got to promise to catch up with Ralph and Linda and not hang around at the back of the group."

"I promise," Nancy said as Ned began to jog ahead. When he reached the curve in the path, he turned and waved, and Nancy waved back.

She wasn't worried—Ralph and Linda were somewhere ahead, within calling distance. But her blister was really beginning to hurt her. Nancy sat down on a rock and unlaced her shoe. Maybe the blister was getting infected. Sure enough, her whole heel was red and inflamed. She would have to try to catch up to Mike, who was carrying the first-aid kit, and see if he had a bandage.

Nancy was lacing her shoe up when she felt that prickle between her shoulder blades—the prickle that always meant she was being watched. She turned around. No one was in sight—but had she heard a rustling in the dense leaves? She got up and began to hurry down the trail, suddenly feeling very vulnerable and wishing that she hadn't let the others get so far ahead.

"Wait!" a rough voice commanded.

Nancy stopped, then turned, her heart in her mouth. There, lurching clumsily toward her through the thick underbrush, was Max! His shirt was ripped in several places, he wore a two-day stubble of beard, and there was an inch-long gash just above his right eye. He carried a heavy tree branch like a club, and his eyes were wild and staring.

Nancy started to run. She had to get away! Max was crazy. He would kill her!

"Don't run!" he shouted, stumbling after her. "I have to talk—"

At that moment, Nancy tripped over a tree root and went sprawling. She struggled back to her feet just as Max reached her.

"You can't get away," he said, panting. "I won't let you!" He swung the club around. That was the last thing Nancy saw before the world went black.

Chapter

Fifteen

FOR A MINUTE Nancy thought the loud chirping in her ears was a noisy bird perched on a branch just over her head. But she soon realized that the sound was coming from inside her head. The side of her head hurt, and she tried to raise her hand to explore the ache with her fingers. But her hands were fastened tightly behind her back!

Without moving a muscle, Nancy opened her eyes cautiously, just enough to see. She was on her side in a clearing. Her back was resting against a granite boulder, and her cheek was pressed against a pillow of pale green moss. The ground was thickly carpeted with pine needles, but whatever Max had used to tie her with was cutting into the circulation at her wrists, and her fingers felt numb.

Max was crouched on the ground five or six feet away, whittling a spearlike point on a long straight stick and coughing intermittently. Nancy closed her eyes and tried to formulate some sort of logical plan of action through the painful throbbing in her head.

She didn't hear any voices. That could either mean the others hadn't yet discovered she was missing or that Max had dragged her so far off the trail that she wasn't able to hear them.

Using her numb fingers, she explored the binding around her wrists. It didn't feel very strong or heavy. Perhaps she could saw through it with a piece of jagged rock. She felt along the boulder at her back. Yes, there was a sharp, protruding seam, where the rock had weathered and split.

Very carefully, she began to push the rope up and down against the seam of the rock, trying not to move her shoulders. She peered surreptitiously through her lashes. Max had raised his head and was listening intently, as if he heard something in the distance. There was a look of fear on his face.

Nancy felt a surge of hope. Maybe Ned and the others were looking for her.

Max got painfully to his feet and picked up his club. When he moved away, out of the line of Nancy's vision, she heard the sound of his footsteps scuffling through the dry leaves and began sawing at the rope frantically.

When her hands came free, Nancy didn't move. Surprise was her only weapon. She had to get Max to come near enough to her so that she could catch him with one unexpected karate blow. But where was he?

In a few minutes, Max returned and leaned over to pick up his crude spear.

"O-oh," Nancy moaned, stirring a little. She could hear Max move toward her. "Nancy?" he said. She moaned again, more faintly this time.

"Nancy?" He bent over her and touched her shoulder. "Are you okay?" he asked in a worried voice. "I didn't mean to hit you so hard, really. I just wanted to talk . . ."

Suddenly Nancy opened her eyes and leaped up. Taken by surprise, Max stumbled back, off balance, his mouth open. Nancy jumped at him, aiming a quick, hard blow to his solar plexus, and Max fell with a loud "Oomph!" He hit his head against a rock and went limp.

Nancy spun away and began to race through the woods. Her head still hurt, and she felt slightly dizzy and disoriented.

She slowed down to a walk, thinking maybe she shouldn't run until she figured out which direction to go in. A puzzled frown came to her face as she remembered Max's words. What was he talking about when he said that he hadn't meant to hurt her—that he just needed to talk? She stopped, hesitating.

"Nancy! Nancy, where are you?" It was Ned's voice, and he sounded frantic. "Nancy!"

"Here, Ned!" Nancy called. "I'm here!" She ran toward the sound of his voice, still calling his name.

"Oh, Nancy!" Breathlessly, Ned burst through a clearing and enveloped her in a huge hug. Bess and George were with him.

"What happened to you? Where have you been all this time?" Bess asked anxiously.

"We told the others we'd be looking for you—Linda was glad to have the rest," George said.

"But, Nan . . ." Ned began.

"What?"

"Why did you leave the trail?"

"I didn't *leave* the trail," Nancy said, feeling the knot on the side of her head. "Max came up behind me and hit me over the head. He carried me pretty far into the woods and tied me up, but I managed to get loose and catch him by surprise. I got away just a few minutes ago."

"Oh, I'm so *glad* you're safe," George said, hugging her. She turned to Bess. "See? I keep telling you Max is dangerous."

Nancy waved her hand to interrupt. "Probably. But there's something that bothers me."

"Bothers you?" Ned asked. "I'd be bothered, too, if somebody knocked me out and tied me up in the middle of the woods."

"Yeah, I know." Nancy sighed. "But Max said something odd, just before I got away. He said that he hadn't meant to hit me so hard, that he just wanted to talk."

"But why would he want to *talk* to you?" Ned asked. "Was he trying to keep you from going to the police?"

Nancy shook her head. "I don't know, but I wish I hadn't hit him so quickly."

Ned considered. "You couldn't take that chance. But we could go back and talk to him now," he suggested. "There're four of us and only one of him."

Nancy looked around. "To tell you the truth, Ned," she confessed, "I don't know which direction I ran after I got away from Max."

Ned followed her scuffed track in the leaves. "It looks like you came from over there," he said, pointing. "Let's go that way."

But even though they searched the woods, they couldn't find the clearing where Max had held Nancy captive. Ned glanced down at his watch.

"It's nearly two o'clock," he said reluctantly. "The others are waiting. We'll have to push hard if we're going to reach the ranger station this afternoon."

"*If* the ranger station is in this direction," Nancy reminded him.

"Right." Ned sighed and took her hand as the four of them headed back to the trail. "If."

"Did you manage to talk to Mercedes?" Nancy asked after a few minutes.

"I tried," Ned answered.

"Oh. No luck?"

"Nope. She wouldn't say a word to me." Ned grinned and squeezed Nancy's hand. "Not even when I turned on some charm."

"Now I really *do* wish I'd had the sense to play possum just a few minutes longer," Nancy said unhappily. "If I'd just listened to Max, he might have given us a clue to this whole thing. I wish—"

"I wish you'd shut up, Detective Drew," Ned said. He slipped his arm affectionately around her shoulders. "It's good to have you safe. Even if you didn't get the clue you wanted."

"He kidnapped you!" Linda exclaimed hysterically when Nancy and her friends finally caught up with the rest of the group and told them what had happened. "He's going to kill us all! He'll track us down and isolate us, one at a time, and kill us."

Ralph rubbed her back. "Don't, Linda," he said helplessly.

Mercedes jumped up. "Maybe Max doesn't

want to hurt the rest of us," she blurted. "Maybe he's just after Nancy."

"No!" Sammy exclaimed. "He's out to kill all of us. I'll bet he's somewhere nearby right now, spying on us, deciding which one of us will be next."

"What do you mean, maybe he was just out after me?" Nancy asked Mercedes. "Why would you think that?"

Mercedes pressed her lips into a tight line. "I don't know," she said. "I was just trying to make Linda feel better, that's all."

Linda began to cry harder, and Sammy looked as if she were going to burst into tears, too. Mercedes's face was closed and dark.

"Listen, everybody," Tod interrupted. "I know we're all tired and sore, but if we don't keep going, we're not going to get to the ranger station before dark."

The climb to the top of the ridge was one of the longest and most wearying hikes that Nancy had ever been on. Her heel was painful, and in spite of the beauty of the mountain, she kept her eyes on the ground, trying to pick out the easiest path. Ahead of her, Linda seemed to moan with every step, and she could hear Sammy complaining bitterly to Mike that they were going the wrong way.

At last they reached the top of the ridge.

"Oh, it's beautiful!" Bess exclaimed. "What a view!"

"And there's the fire tower!" Tod said triumphantly, pointing along the ridge to the left. "It's only a half-mile or so away!"

"All right!" Ralph let loose a giant whoop.

"Hey, wait a minute," Nancy said, her wide grin fading. "If the tower's deserted, will it still have a radio? We can still get a message out, can't we?"

"Yup," Tod assured her, "and the Forest Service will send a helicopter for us—probably before sunset! Of course, they'll have to send a team in to look for Paula's body."

With the ranger station so close, the group seemed a great deal more relaxed. Even Linda managed a smile when a small brown fawn hopped across the trail in front of them.

"I don't see any signs of life," Ned observed when they reached the station. Beside the trail stood a small cabin with a sign on it reading United States Forest Service, but grass was growing up in front of the door—the cabin seemed to be deserted.

"How do they get people and supplies up here?" Sammy wanted to know. "I don't see any roads."

"There *aren't* roads to some of these back-country towers," Mike replied. "That's why they use helicopters."

"So that's the tower," Bess said, looking across the yard that separated it from the station. It was a squat, square box built on stilts forty feet in the air, with a stair zigzagging between the stilts. Halfway up was an open platform. "I'll bet there's a good view from up there."

"You're right," Mike told her. "Since these lookout towers are built so that rangers can watch for fires, they have an unobstructed view of the whole country." He grinned. "Want to take a look? I'm going to go up and get that message out."

"We'll all go," Sammy decided.

"I'm not sure I can climb that high," Linda objected.

"You'll never have another chance like this one," Ralph told her.

"Oh, okay."

"Well, then, let's go," Mike said, and they started toward the tower.

Suddenly George clutched Nancy's sleeve. "Nancy! I saw somebody run behind that building over there!"

Nancy turned to see a blur of movement behind one of the rickety wooden sheds only a few yards away.

Linda gasped. "It's Max!" she cried when the figure stepped out and started toward them. "He's coming to kill us!"

Chapter

Sixteen

"LET'S GET HIM!" Tod shouted.

"Watch out," Mike cautioned. "He's got a club."

"That's okay," Tod said, his eyes narrowed to slits. "We can handle that."

"Wait," Ned said. "I think he just wants to talk."

But Tod and Mike ignored Ned and advanced threateningly toward Max.

"Hold on," Max rasped. He kept walking toward them. His shoulders slumped wearily, and he seemed to be dragging one foot. "I don't want to hurt anybody. All I want is to talk to Nancy."

"Then put that club down," Ned said reasonably, stepping forward and holding out both hands to show that they were empty. "Nobody's got any weapons here. Nancy will talk to you if you throw your weapon away."

"Not on your life," Max said with a gesture toward Tod and Mike.

He lifted the stick, and Nancy could see that he had driven a giant, lethal-looking spike into the end of it. "Stay back!" he rasped when Tod moved closer. "Where's Nancy Drew? It's a matter of life and death!" A shadow of pain crossed his face, and he began to cough.

"Here I am," Nancy said, stepping forward beside Ned. She could hear Max's harsh, labored breathing. "What do you want?"

For an instant, distracted by Nancy's voice and by his own coughing, Max lowered the stick. Mike and Tod rushed him. Mike tackled him around the knees, bringing him down, and Tod tried to pin his arms behind his back. Max fought back with the strength of a madman, and the three rolled on the dusty ground in a silent, violent tangle. But after a moment, the two were too much for Max, and Tod managed to get astride him. He put his hands around Max's neck, trying to throttle him.

"Ned!" Nancy screamed, running toward them. "Stop him! We've *got* to hear what Max has to say! He may be our key to this mystery!"

Ned jumped in with the skill that made him

Emerson's star quarterback. He grabbed Mike by the collar and tossed him several feet away. But as he reached for Tod, Tod jumped up and picked up the club Max had dropped.

"Now I've got you!" Tod shouted down at Max. "You're not going to get away with killing Paula!" He poised to strike, the spike glinting viciously at the end of the stick.

Suddenly Nancy lashed out with a hard, flying kick at the small of Tod's back. As she struck him, the club was knocked out of his hands and he fell to the ground, gasping.

Max had raised himself to his hands and knees, trying painfully to push himself up off the ground. Blood oozed out of the corner of his mouth. The gash over his right eye had opened up again. His other eye was already puffed and swelling where Tod had hit him. Max crouched and fell forward.

Ned took off his canvas belt and bent over Max, hauling him up to a sitting position. "I'm not going to hurt him, I'm just going to make sure he doesn't get away," he told Nancy. He pulled Max's arms behind his back and looped the belt twice around his forearms, before he pushed it through the buckle and cinched it tight.

Helplessly, Max dropped his head between his knees. Nancy leaned over him. It sounded as if he were trying to say something.

"It wasn't me!" he said, sucking in his breath

with a hollow, whistling sound. "I didn't . . . I didn't kill Paula!"

"What?" Nancy and Ned said together.

Max coughed again. "It . . . it was the other way around," he gasped, attempting to pull himself up straight. "She . . ." His eyes glazed over, and he fell heavily to his side in the dirt. "Be careful," he whispered to Nancy, his voice fading. "She's after you!"

"After me? But why? What are you trying to say, Max?"

"She's trying to kill you. She's not . . . she's not . . ." Max's head fell back limply.

Ned felt for a pulse. "He's passed out," he said grimly.

Nancy stared up at Ned. "Do you suppose he was telling the truth?" she asked. "That he *didn't* kill Paula?"

"Max!" Bess came running up. She had ripped off the tail of her blouse and soaked it in water from the canteen. She knelt down beside Max and began to wipe the blood off his face. "Is he going to be all right?" she asked fearfully.

Ned stood up after freeing Max's hands. "It's hard to say," he replied, looking down on Max's unconscious face. "He's probably got some internal injuries—maybe some broken ribs, maybe worse." He scowled at Tod and Mike. "The beating didn't help any."

Tod hung his head. "It looked like he was

going to try to get away. We were just making sure he didn't." Tod glanced up again. "What did he mean when he said he didn't kill Paula?"

"Maybe there was somebody *else* up there with them?" Mike said. "I don't know—do you suppose somebody else pushed Paula over the cliff?"

"And what about his warning to you?" Ned asked Nancy, with a puzzled look. "When Max said that Paula is out to kill you, he was talking like she's still alive!"

"That's impossible," Tod scoffed. "We *saw* her fall from the cliff and into the water."

Nancy shook her head, frowning. "We'll have to wait until Max regains consciousness to be sure that's what happened. Then we can ask him some more questions."

"There's a shed over there," Ned said, pointing toward a group of weathered, ramshackle outbuildings. "And I see a folded-up tarp just inside the door. Let's put Max on the tarp and move him into the shed, where he'll be out of this sun."

It took a few minutes to move Max. The others stood silently, watching, as if they were afraid Max might come to and attack them.

When Max was lying on the floor of the shed, Mike straightened up and dusted off his hands, looking at his watch. "I'm going to go up to the tower and send off that message," he said. "It's nearly three o'clock now. If we don't let the rangers know right away that we're here, they might not be able to get us out before dark."

Nancy, Ned, and Bess decided to stay with Max while the others climbed the tower with Mike. They had been gone for five minutes or so when Max began to stir.

"Max," Nancy said urgently, bending over him. "Can you talk? Who pushed Paula over the cliff? Was somebody else up there with you?"

Max didn't answer. After opening his eyes he just stared, then lapsed into a delirious sleep.

"Oh," Bess moaned, twisting her fingers anxiously. "He looks like he's going to die."

"I'm going to go after Mike and tell him to ask the Forest Service to send a doctor with the helicopter," Nancy said suddenly, scrambling to her feet. She pulled out the tiny notebook and pencil that she always carried and handed it to Ned. "If he says anything you can understand—even if it sounds like nonsense—write it down."

"Okay," Ned promised.

Nancy started across the dusty yard of the ranger station toward the tower. She was deep in thought. Max had said that *he* didn't kill Paula. "It was the other way around," he had said. But that could only mean one thing: That Paula had tried to kill him!

The wind picked up suddenly, moaning around the tower.

Nancy began to climb the stairs. She was

partway up when she caught a flash of movement below her. A slight figure dashed out of the dense woods that surrounded the ranger station and ran across the yard toward the tower. Staring unbelievingly at the runner, who had already begun to take the stairs toward her, two at a time, Nancy gripped the steel railing.

"Paula!" she gasped.

Chapter

Seventeen

Yes, it's me," Paula said, panting and out of breath. She clattered up the stairs toward Nancy. Her long hair was matted and full of twigs and brambles, her cold amber eyes wild and staring. In that instant, Nancy realized that Paula was insane.

"What do you want?" She held Paula's eyes with her own as she gingerly backed up the stairs.

"I want you," Paula said over the roar of the wind. "You're the one I've been after all along. I'm going to kill you!"

Nancy sensed that if she could keep Paula talking, she might be able to distract her. At least she could stave off an attack for a few minutes until Paula was in a position where she could be overpowered.

"Why are you trying to kill me?" Nancy said. "I don't even know you."

"Are you sure?" Paula asked, baring her teeth in a smile. Her amber eyes glittered like the eyes of the rattlesnake. She came up another step. "Does the name Peter Hancock mean anything to you?"

"Peter Hancock?" Nancy was genuinely puzzled. "No," she said. "Why should it?" And then she remembered. Suddenly she knew where she had seen those strange amber eyes.

Peter Hancock was the name of an embezzler who had worked as an accountant at a bank in New York. It had been Nancy's careful detective work that had uncovered his fraudulent activities and sent him to prison.

Menacingly, Paula stepped closer. "Peter Hancock was my father. *You* sent him to prison, and now he's dead!" Paula's eyes were gleaming. "He escaped a few months ago. But he died—in this very wilderness. And you're going to die here, too!"

"So," Nancy said quickly, "you rigged this whole thing to get me here."

"That's right," Paula replied, brushing a strand of her matted hair out of her eyes. "There wasn't any contest—just like there wasn't any White Water Rafting, Incorporated.

Both those tricks were part of a plan to get you on the river, where I could teach you a lesson, once and for all."

"So you picked your winners at random?"

"Yes," Paula bragged.

"Well, that was smart," Nancy said, stalling. If only the group on top of the tower could hear her above the wind! "People are always putting their names into a box for one contest or another. I guess you figured they'd think they'd just forgotten about entering this one."

"You got it, Nancy Drew." Paula sneered. "You're bright, all right. Too bad you're not bright enough to get yourself out of the mess you're in now."

Nancy ignored her. "And you sent the letter to George because you knew that she'd be enthusiastic about white water rafting trip," Nancy prompted.

"Of course I knew it. I've been doing my homework. I know all about you and your friends. It was a sure thing that George Fayne would ask you to come on this trip with her."

"The map? The missing barricade?"

"They were easy," Paula said scornfully. "You know, you would have made a lot less trouble for me if you'd sailed off that cliff." She sighed. "But I'm glad those tricks didn't work. It's going to be a lot more fun to watch you die."

"What about the slipped mooring line?"

Nancy asked before Paula could make a move. "Was that another one of your clever tricks?"

"I figured it would be interesting to watch the expressions on your friends' faces when we fished your body out from under the falls," Paula explained. She stepped up closer to Nancy. "But I'm getting tired of all this talk."

Nancy retreated a step higher. Just three or four more steps and she'd be on the tower's lower platform. If she could lure Paula up there, she might be able to maneuver her into a more vulnerable position. "Max—" Nancy said, "was he in on your plan?"

Paula gave a disdainful laugh. "Not at all—at least not until he began to figure out what was going on. Of course, I didn't count on his capsizing the raft—"

"I guess that was a stroke of good luck for you," Nancy put in. "It put one of the rafts out of commission. When that happened, you probably thought it would be a better idea to get me off into the woods and kill me there."

"Very impressive brainwork, Detective Drew. When the first raft was destroyed, I had to finish off the other one, too—to keep you from going downriver the next morning. And I nearly did get you in the woods."

"You certainly did. If it hadn't been for Ned—"

"The boulder would have crushed you," Paula finished. She smiled cruelly.

"You know, I've got to admire you," Nancy said, grudgingly. "We actually thought *you* were dead—that Max had killed you and was out to kill us, too. I bet I know how you arranged that," Nancy said.

"I don't care if you know or not," Paula snapped, her face twisting. She lunged for Nancy, surprising her.

Nancy took two steps up and back but couldn't escape Paula's grasp on her arm. They fell together onto the wooden deck of the platform. Nancy felt Paula's elbow dig into her side. She rolled onto her back and raised her feet, catching Paula's shoulders. Then she shoved as hard as she could.

With a howl of rage, Paula launched herself forward from the railing. "I'm going to kill you!" she shouted, but this time Nancy was ready for her. As Paula rushed with full force, Nancy sidestepped adroitly and tripped her.

For an instant, Paula's arms flailed wildly. Then she crashed against the weather-beaten wood. There was a splintering sound as the railing gave way under her weight. She tried to catch herself. Then, in a clumsy slow-motion swan dive, she fell over the edge, screaming.

The scream broke off, and Nancy looked over the splintered railing. Paula was sprawled face-up and motionless on the concrete apron at the foot of the tower, one arm bent under her, eyes staring up at the sky.

The wind had died down. The air was perfectly still.

From the contorted position in which Paula lay, Nancy knew Paula was dead.

"Hey! What's going on down there?"

Nancy looked above her and saw Sammy peering down at Paula's sprawled body. Sammy looked as if she were seeing a ghost. "Is Paula really dead?" Sammy asked.

Bess was kneeling next to the body, feeling for a pulse. "I think so," she called up soberly.

Nancy leaned weakly against the solid part of the railing until Ned streaked up the stairs and pulled her into his arms. After clinging together for a moment or two, they followed the group, who had just raced down from the lookout tower.

"I don't understand," Linda said. "How did Paula survive the fall from the cliff?"

"She never fell off the cliff. Max did—or, rather, he was—"

"Pushed."

It was Max's voice. Nancy looked up. Max was leaning against the doorjamb of the shed.

Ned and Tod hurried over to Max and helped him walk across the yard.

Bess approached him anxiously. "Are you sure you're up to this? The helicopter is bringing a doctor in a little while."

"I'm all right," Max said weakly, but his breathing came in jagged gasps.

143

"Paula pushed you—is that what you're saying?" Ralph asked in astonishment. "But we heard Paula shout. . . . And we saw . . ." He stopped. "Oh, I see," he said. "Paula faked it—the shout and everything."

Ned's arm had been around Nancy. "You're trembling," he said to her. "Are you cold? Do you want to borrow my jacket again?"

Nancy gave one last nervous shiver. Then all at once she smiled at Ned. "No, thanks," she said, as if she had a secret. She turned to Max. "But that's what Paula did, didn't she, Max—give you her jacket?" Max nodded weakly and tried to talk. "Let me tell it," Nancy said.

"When you got to the top of the cliff, you confronted Paula with what you knew, and then you got into a big argument. She distracted you and knocked you over the head with something —a rock maybe?"

"Yes," Max said, fingering the gash over his eye.

"And when you fell," Nancy went on, "that's when we heard the thump. The jacket—now that was a clever move on Paula's part, since she knew I'd be on my guard against her every second if I thought she'd pushed *you* off the cliff. That's why she had to make believe *she* was the victim.

"And until I remembered that Ned had loaned me his jacket, she almost had me fooled.

It took me a while, but suddenly I realized how easy it would have been for her to put her jacket on you—it was big enough."

Max coughed and spoke. "The trick boomer-anged, though. Her jacket is what saved my life. It was so big, air got trapped in it and helped keep me afloat until I could grab on to a limb and pull myself out."

Wincing in pain, he sank to the ground. "But I think I broke a couple of ribs in the fall."

Bess knelt beside him and wiped away the beads of sweat on his forehead.

Sammy looked from Max to Paula's body. "But why did Paula do it? Was she responsible for holing the raft and stealing the crystal out of the radio?"

"Paula was responsible for everything," Nancy said. "She invented the contest—"

"Invented the contest?" Mike exclaimed.

"Yes, it was a trick to get *me* here."

"See?" Linda said smugly to Ralph. "I told you the whole thing had to be a joke."

"Some joke," George said bitterly. She turned to Nancy. "But I don't understand why Paula did all this."

"Revenge," Nancy replied simply, and she told everyone the story of Peter Hancock.

"So she didn't care who else got hurt in the process," Tod put in, shaking his head.

"You're right," Max said, sounding the

slightest bit stronger. "On the cliff, she said she was going to kill me because I knew too much. And she told me she'd kill everybody else if she had to—just to get to Nancy Drew." He turned to Nancy with a lopsided grin. "That's what I was trying to tell you when I pulled you into the woods this morning. I didn't mean to knock you out. I just wanted to warn you about Paula."

"I wasn't sure about the mooring line," Max went on, "but I saw her push the boulder down on you yesterday—"

"You did?"

"Yeah, and when I saw you walking by yourself, I figured it would be a good time to let you know about the danger you were in."

Nancy looked at Max curiously. "When did you realize what was going on?" she asked. "Was it before you saw Paula take the compass?"

"I guess it was when I began to suspect that she was the one who holed the raft," Max answered. "You see, when you told me you were a detective, I suddenly remembered I'd seen your picture in the local newspaper after Peter Hancock's trial.

"I realized then that you were the person who'd blown the whistle on Paula's father. And yesterday morning, when Paula made the crack about the 'famous girl detective,' I began to suspect that she had it in for you."

"Hmm," said Nancy. "You didn't suspect Paula till yesterday? Then you couldn't have been the person who made the phone call warning me not to take this trip, could you have, Max?" Nancy turned slowly to Mercedes. Mercedes stepped forward wearily. "You were trying to protect Paula, isn't that right?" Nancy asked her gently.

Mercedes broke into tears. "If you'd known her before her father died, you would understand—" She looked up. "I'm so sorry, Nancy. I never wanted you to get hurt—or anyone else, either. Really."

"How did you know what Paula was planning?" Nancy asked.

"Well, I knew how unbalanced Paula had been since my uncle Peter died—you know, they found his body only a few miles from here. Anyway, I found your name on the list of 'contest winners' that Paula gave me when she told me about the trip."

Nancy frowned. "Didn't you question her?"

"Sure I did, but she said she just wanted to teach you a little lesson. I called you just in case, I guess. I thought the call might make you bring along some extra protection."

"Ah," Nancy said. "That's why you were snooping around in my pack—you were trying to see if I had a weapon or something, to scare Paula with it if I had to."

Mercedes nodded tearfully. "Sort of. But I don't know what I would have done if I'd found one. I wanted to protect you, but I wanted to protect Paula, and after she was dead, I didn't think there was any point—"

"—in dragging up the past," Nancy finished.

Ned got the tarp out of the shed and covered up Paula's body. "She must have been crazy with grief over her father's death," he said grimly.

"She was," Mercedes said, sobbing heavily. "She was."

"I think we were *all* a little crazy," George said later that afternoon as they boarded one of the helicopters that came to pick them up.

"Maybe next time you'll listen," Bess said, trying to comb the tangles out of her hair with her fingers. "We could have been sunning ourselves for the last three days." Then she brightened. "But I think I've lost five pounds." She glanced toward the front of the helicopter where Max was lying on a stretcher. "And I've met Max. So it wasn't a total loss."

Ned settled himself next to Nancy. "It wasn't a romantic holiday," he said softly to her, "but at least I had you in sight the whole time."

Nancy sighed, thinking of how scratched and bitten she must look. "Yes, and *what* a sight."

"Well, you know what they say about love," Ned said, laughing.

"No, what's that?" Nancy asked, raising her voice over the clatter of the helicopter engines.

"Love is blind," Ned shouted into her ear, and leaned over to kiss her.

"It's a good thing!" Nancy exclaimed, and kissed him back.

Nancy's next case:

Nancy is excited about this assignment—undercover work at a women's tennis tournament. It's a chance to work on an interesting case *and* watch some great tennis with Bess and George. But Nancy doesn't realize she'll end up trapped in an off-the-court nightmare.

The star of the tournament, Teresa Montenegro, looks just like Nancy. It's quite a coincidence—a deadly coincidence. Someone wants Teresa out of the way, and the killer's having a tough time telling the two girls apart.

When Teresa's boyfriend is killed, the ball is definitely in Nancy's court. Can she save Teresa from an international terrorist without becoming a target herself? Find out in *DEADLY DOUBLES*, Case #7 in *The Nancy Drew Files*™.